Dedicated to you.

SILENCE IN THE BASEMENT

ALEX MURA

HANABI PRESS

Hanabi Press
London

www.alexmura.com

This paperback edition 2024
10 9 8 7 6 5 4 3 2 1

ISBN: 978-1-0686575-1-1 (paperback)
ISBN 978-1-0686575-0-4 (ebook)

This novel is entirely a work of fiction.
The names, characters, and incidents portrayed in it are
the work of the author's imagination. Any resemblance to
actual persons, living or dead, events or localities is
entirely coincidental.

1

A set of sirens shriek and I catch the blue and red lights of a cop car in the mirror. Muttering under my breath, I pull over and slow my truck to a stop. Takes a minute before this young cop comes up and signals me to roll down the window.

"Afternoon, officer."

"Afternoon, sir," he replies, nice and firm. He's a clean-cut guy, hair slicked back, not a whisker on his face. You know what they say about cops looking younger the older you get? "License and registration, please?"

I have no reason to make a fuss, so I hand over the papers from the glove box. Best to comply, so I can go about my day sooner. He takes them and tells me to hang tight. As he walks away, I nudge the radio volume up, filling the silence with a classic tune, a favorite of mine. I hum along quietly, easing the bubbling in my stomach. Why does authority always make me feel like I did something wrong?

He returns soon enough. "Thanks for waiting, Mr. Griffin," he says. "Just a routine check. Doing them all along the highway, so don't be surprised if you get pulled over again."

"No problem. Just doing your job, I'm sure."

He subtly raises his eyebrows, as if he expected me to show some curiosity. I guess most people don't like to mind their own business so much these days. Perhaps it's easier if I play along, but I don't really care why he pulled me over. I just want to be on my way.

"Did something happen out here?"

He nods. "We've had a series of unexplained disappearances across the state. Been told they were all traveling along Route 50 at some point around the time they went missing."

"Reckon they were kidnapped?" I ask, my curiosity piqued now. I'm not the sort of guy to beat around the bush.

"Not sure yet," the cop says, "We're investigating whether there's a connection, but people vanish without a trace all the time round these parts. Could all be runaways, as they're all quite young."

"Well, I guess I don't need to worry then, but I'll keep an eye out."

The cop nods but takes a step closer to my window. "Just watch out while you are out there, okay? Better safe than sorry. We found a car for sale in town. It belonged to one of the missing kids. The dealership manager claimed it just showed up one morning, parked on the lot with a note under the wiper saying 'take me.' Struck me as pretty darn strange, if you ask me."

"If I spot anything out of the ordinary, you boys will be the first to know," I say with a polite nod.

"Appreciate it," the cop says, smiling now for the first time. It knocks a few more years off him until he can't be long out of his teens. He hands back my papers and heads back to his cruiser. Over his shoulder, he says, "Drive safe."

Always do, officer. Always do.

The cop's words echo around my brain as I put my truck into gear and head on out. *People vanish all the time.* They just run off or end it all. But a car turning up with a note on it? Who does that? Alarm bells are ringing, but it ain't my business. Still, as I return to cruising speed on the highway, I can't help chewing it over. If it was a suicide, then there has to be a body, right? This place is as empty as it gets; no houses, no nothing. There aren't so many places a kidnapper could hide.

While the roads are clear on both sides with good visibility ahead, I glance up to the two pictures taped on the sun visor. Olivia and Sally. My two angels. I tap them both for luck and return my eyes to the road. Nowadays, my truck, Midnight, is all I have left in my life. She's my fortress of solitude. Sitting here in the driver's seat, hands wrapped around the steering wheel, *this* is my home, not the crummy place where I live—if you even call it living.

3

There's nothing ahead except this long stretch of road, with only miles of desert and some distant mountains for company. Just me and the occasional car that zooms past. Route 50 sure lives up to its name—the Loneliest Road in America. But I don't mind. In fact, I think I like it better that way. The familiarity is comforting. The quiet is only broken by the steady growl of my truck's engine and the wind hitting its windows. Good thing I've got my country music. I crank up the radio and there's my favorite country trio, playing only for me. I can't help but sing along, tapping my hand on my knee to the beat. The music stops me mulling over the disappearances that young cop fella told me about. Poor parents of those missing kids. I know how that feels and it ain't nice. Besides, I don't need bad omens looming over me.

As the tune wraps up, I reach over and grab my coffee-filled thermal cup from the door pocket. It's still hot. Man, how much I love that first sip! But looks like I'm running low, just like with the gas. A few miles further down I pass a worn sign that reads *gas station - eleven miles*. I guess I'll stop there, fuel up, and stretch my legs.

I pick and choose which jobs I want to do, which ones I don't. I'm my own boss, and that's exactly the way I like it. Right now, I'm hauling clothes for some fancy brand I've never heard of. Can't even remember the damn name, but it's probably something the kids wear. I guess that's what happens when you're not a spring chicken anymore.

Just passed the city of Ely in Nevada. Roughly four hundred miles left until I reach Sacramento. The weather is clear, and the traffic is non-existent, so I'm on track to reach my destination a day or two early. I can't wait to finish this run. Once it's done and dusted, I'm heading back to Texas for a couple of well-earned weeks off. It's been two whole years since I last took a proper break. I'm beat. Even a road dog like me needs to rest. Just a shame the only thing I'll be coming back to is an empty home, my country records, and a fridge full of beer.

Glancing up, my eyes land again on the photographs taped to the sun visor. A grin spreads across my dumb face. That honeymoon with Sally was the best week of my life. Before Olivia came along, of course. A memory surfaces of the two of us, soaking up the sun with the hot sand between our toes, seagulls squawking overhead, and a bunch of other people's kids running wild, building sandcastles. It was a heck of a change from my little town in Texas, that's for sure. Sally said she'd never seen me smile so much. She looked beautiful in that floral linen dress I bought her, with her hair all tied up. And me? I was stuck in these ridiculous blue shark-print trunks I bought from some beach store—left my own at home. Sally got a real kick out of them. Was she teasing me? Who knows, but I'll never grow tired thinking about it.

The smile doesn't last long, though. It never does.

I drive on autopilot, hands and feet doing their own thing while my mind drifts. It happens a lot, daydreaming. Sometimes it's good stuff, like now. But mostly, not so much. I've always been a loner; guess that's why I took to trucking. There is no need for small talk or pretending to care. Just me and the open road. Although, being stuck in my own head day after day takes its toll. It would be a nice change to have someone to talk to, someone to call a friend. Companionship.

I crank up the radio until the speakers rattle, and I can only feel the steady bass thrum of Midnight's engine, not hear it. The country tunes drown out everything, even my thoughts. These radio deejays never let me down. They play the good stuff and even take requests. I call in so often they know me by name.

"And now, let's hear some requests from y'all," the radio sputters. "Just dial our toll-free number on—"

I'm already on it. I'm on hold with the station, hands free, of course. They pick up and I turn down the radio. My heart skips a beat, being live on air. "Hey," I say, keeping it short.

"I know that voice!" The host sounds excited. "Hank, right?"

"Yep, it's me." I don't care much for the small talk, but I gotta admit, it's a thrill picking a tune for everyone's enjoyment. Being a deejay must be a real hoot.

"For those just tuning in, Hank here's a genuine regular," the host announces. "Always picks a winner. What's it gonna be today, buddy?"

I request "Amarillo by Morning" by George Strait. It's one of those classics that never gets old. The host thanks me and soon Strait's familiar tune fills the cabin. I turn the volume up, losing myself in the song, picturing Sally beside me, her voice harmonizing with mine.

My eyes catch a reflection in the side mirror. My beard's getting thicker with every trim. It's well-kept, but it's beginning to get a little too raggedy for my liking. My hair, usually short, brushes over my ears now, and I've started using some cheap hair product to keep it swept backwards out of my eyes. Sally used to wonder how I'd look with longer hair. Guess she'd be pleasantly surprised. I try to keep a respectable appearance, like now, but some weeks I just don't give a rat's ass. Truth is, it's hard to care when there's nobody to impress.

My stomach growls, reminding me I haven't eaten since yesterday. Glancing at the time, I realize that it's already nearing one o'clock. The highway takes me down a few more miles across the empty stretch of road until I finally see a truck-stop. I pull in, joining two other truckers and grab some stuff from the cab—a foldable chair, some vegetables, a two-liter water bottle, and utensils from the cab.

Taking the steps down to the pavement, my body reacts as if I'm an astronaut coming back to earth after a year in space. My legs nearly give in, but I lock my knees just in time. I give the other truckers a quick glance, then slowly head round to the side of Midnight. I don't tend to talk much with folks in the business. Ain't nothing worth talking about. There's a small latch on the truck. I put everything down, then pull the latch sideways, allowing a small table to fold out—my makeshift dining area.

Once everything's set up, I take a second to stretch my legs out properly. They've been cramped behind the wheel for fifteen hours straight. That explains why my eyelids are heavy. I've been pushing myself to wrap this job up as quickly as I can, ignoring my usual routine and the HOS guidelines on driving more than eleven hours straight. It's time to call it a day.

In normal circumstances, I drive from nine in the evening to seven in the morning. There's less traffic, no noise, more peace. I've always been drawn to the night. It's like a therapist that you don't have to pay. I will admit, falling asleep on highways during the day was hard for the first six months or so, but now I sleep like a log.

Seeing the ingredients I have laid out boosts my spirits again. I chop up onion, garlic, leek, celery, and potatoes, tossing them into a pot of water. I chuck in a stock cube too, some seasoning, and light up the gas stove. The aroma of the stew as it boils is just perfect. I stir it, then let it simmer on low heat, covered. It really is freeing, being able to just stop whenever I see fit, and get some grub in me. I feel sorry for the drones, working their nine-to-fives, eyeing their watches like hawks, waiting for their thirty minutes of freedom. Their bosses probably time their toilet break. Only the availability of truck stops defines when I get to take a dump, but ain't nobody telling me how long I spend in there.

The other truckers have congregated near their trucks, their chatter and laughter disturbing my peace. When they glance over, I offer a friendly nod and a smile, but don't engage. To my relief, they understand the message and leave me be. Honest to God, anyone from any other occupation I meet on the road, I'll at least exchange pleasantries. But me and other truckers aren't a great mix.

I sink into the quiet again, waiting for my stew to boil with George Strait's voice keeping me company. The December air bites a little. It's not too bad, though; maybe around twelve degrees. Although the nights here get downright frosty. I button up my checkered overshirt and shuffle my hands closer to the stove for warmth.

Thoughts roll around in my head. I'm fifty-four now. Ten more years to sixty-four, if I'm aiming to retire. I don't mind the work, but what nags me is whether I've saved enough to enjoy some quiet years. Health-wise, I'm holding up alright. Sure, I smoke a few cigarettes each day and drink my share of beer, but I keep fit. Fifty push-ups and sit-ups every day—I reckon I could hit eighty-four, easy.

However, there's this nagging debt. Maybe I could sell the ranch, settle down somewhere cheap. But that's no life, is it? On the bad days, I think maybe I'd like to join my two girls sooner, rather than later.

Then, like a ghost, a memory takes hold. The first time I heard her voice. I'm back in the truck, barreling down the highway. The speedometer climbs—fifty, sixty, seventy. I slam the pedal down, feeling Midnight shake with the effort. It's dark, but I spot the headlights of an oncoming truck. Steadily, I start drifting over the line, into the other lane. The other truck blares its horn desperately, which I tune out. I'm ready for it, ready to leave it all behind. Ready to join them.

But then, Sally's voice calls out as clear as day. "Hank," she says. "It's not your time. Not yet."

My heart races, instincts yanking the wheel back just in time. I miss the other truck by a hair and am left shaking, the sound of its horn still ringing in my ears.

Snapping back to reality, I realize I've been leaning into the steam from the pot. It's been near a year since that day, and she comes to me from time to time, usually when I'm at my lowest. I switch off the stove and give it a stir. My stomach's rumbling its own tune.

"Bon appétit," I mutter, scooping up a spoonful. It's still boiling hot, but I hold it in, letting the heat dance across my tongue before finally swallowing. It hurts, but there's something satisfying about it. I polish off both portions of the stew, savoring every bite.

While I clean between my teeth with my nails, I lean back and gaze out at the desert, empty, except for the scattered pinyon pines and sagebrush. Off in the distance, the Sierra mountains stand tall. They're peaceful, more so than any movie could capture. A sudden urge hits me to climb those snowy peaks, look down at this road, and my truck, tiny from up so high. Yeah, I'll put that on my bucket list.

Maybe I should crash here for the night, but those other truckers are making a racket. Their laughter's like nails on a chalkboard. I'm sure I'll find another truck stop further down, need to fuel up anyway. I run my fingers through my hair, scratching my scalp—man, that feels good. After I tidy up my makeshift kitchen, I climb back into Midnight, start her up, and rev her engine.

The radio's back on—country music, my constant companion who never leaves me. The sun's dipping lower now, the dashboard clock says three o'clock.

2

A few miles down, the fluorescent sign of a gas station catches my eye. I pull in and start refueling, letting it fill up all the way so that I don't have to make any further stops. While I'm at it, my eyes catch a couple at the next pump, loud as hell. Hillbillies, by the looks of them, and not the good sort. The guy's dressed in grubby overalls, all skin and bones. His partner's no prize either, in a wrinkled polka-dot dress and with hair springing out in all directions, a wild mix of grey and brown. They're bickering like there's no tomorrow and only pause for a moment when they catch me staring. I instinctively lower my gaze and concentrate on the gasoline pump.

"Ey, watcha lookin' at, pal?" the man hollers.

I ignore him. He's just looking for trouble—something I have no interest in entertaining. I finish up, jamming the pump back into its holder, and hear him stomping over. Fortunately, his missus calls him back, while simultaneously hurling insults my way. They head into the store, and I follow, trying to keep a low profile. I just wanna get to Sacramento and be done with my delivery so I can get home for some rest.

The guy spits on the ground as he opens the door. Brown watery phlegm. Disgusting habit. Inside, I pretend to browse the well-stocked chips aisle, waiting for them to clear out. The couple stand there for a good minute, bickering about which scratch cards to buy. When they finally pay up, I duck, pretending to look at the lower section of the isle when the hillbilly guy turns around and spots me. Bad luck. He strolls over and leans in.

"Watch who you look at," he mutters. "Next time, you won't be so lucky."

Up close, he's even rougher, and the stench is something else entirely. I just nod, keeping my eyes on the ground until he leaves. Cowering, I can't help but feel sorry for myself. I've changed a lot. I used to think fighting was the way forward, but now, at fifty-four, I know better. Ever since hitting my thirties, I've always believed that talking things out beats settling an argument with your fists any day. Violence is just a weak man's game. Nobody wins in a street fight. But truth be told, even a bit of verbal sparring gets my nerves up. So much for being a Griffin. My Daddy would be ashamed.

As I walk up to the counter with a bag of chips that I didn't even realize I'd grabbed, the cashier lets out a deep sigh, unable to hide the fed-up look on his face. "I can't stand those two," he says, shaking his head. "Act like they own the place. Good for nothin' hillbillies."

"They come by often?" I ask.

"Way too often," he says. "Always lurking around. Only thing nearby is that motel a few miles out. Eldorado, I think it's called. Quaint little spot. Dunno what that pair does around here, to be frank with ya. Whatever it is, ain't no good coming from it."

I'm nodding along, but a yawn sneaks out. "Yeah, they're quite the characters."

The cashier nods back. "You look beat," he observes. "If you're heading west, maybe give that motel a shot. It ain't much, but a bed is all ya need, right?"

I purse my lips. "Appreciate the advice, friend."

"Drive safe now," the cashier calls after me as I walk out. Second person to tell me that recently after the cop. Do I look like someone who isn't a good driver?

Stepping outside, I watch the couple peel off down the road in their clunker of a pickup truck. It leaves a trail of thick black smoke, but not enough to obscure the woman flipping me off as they chug past. I just frown after them till they're out of sight. Another yawn hits me. I usually bunk in the truck, but now, I'm fighting to keep my eyes open. Maybe a night at a motel ain't such a bad idea, long as there's room for Midnight.

Radio on and Sally's photo smiling at me from the visor, I head off, my sagging bones looking forward to some proper rest.

Not ten minutes go by when the Eldorado Motel hoves into view. It's clear that it has seen better days. The half-lit sign reads 'El-or-do,' and the paint is so worn it's hard to make out what color it's supposed to be. It's certainly not my idea of a five-star rest stop, but anything with a bed and four walls beats sleeping in the truck. My neck will thank me, anyway. At least if the growing crook is anything to go by.

The motel is a standard L-shaped setup, boasting five or six rooms on each side. There's a courtyard in the middle that looks cared for, with a big pinyon pine and some benches scattered around.

As I'm scoping out a parking spot for Midnight, this kid bolts out of the reception.

"Stop!" he blares out. "Go 'round the back for parking." He points me in the right direction.

I give him a nod and reverse. Kid's voice is kinda high-pitched, and he's got this bored look, wearing a graphic tee and hair all over the place. Bet I've got a bunch of shirts like that in the back of Midnight.

There's a dirt road behind the place. Perfect. I steer Midnight in and park her, then stroll into reception and ask the kid wearing the graphic tee for a room.

"Thirty bucks a night," he says.

15

I peel off three tens from my billfold and hand over the cash, already looking forward to hitting the hay. The reception kid sticks to the basics, and I'm grateful for it. He's young, probably just clocking hours for cash. Doubt he gives enough of a shit to pry into my business.

"Name?" he asks.

"Hank Griffin."

"Like the boxer?"

"Just like the boxer."

Not me, but my father. He was pretty well known, at least in our small corner of America. He was so proud of his accomplishments that he named me after him. Unfortunately, all that brawling left him with brain trauma, like most boxers of a certain vintage. Perhaps that explains why violence always turned me off.

"Hello? The kid's voice brings me back, waving his hand in front of my face.

"Yeah."

"How long?"

I stifle a yawn. "Just for tonight."

The kid jots my details in an old ledger and hands me a key. "Room ten," he says.

"Thanks."

"One thing," the kid says as I turn around. "Bring the keys back to reception when you leave. I'm sick of people leaving them in their damn rooms."

"Understood," I say. "Guess common sense is a rare commodity these days."

"Round here, it sure is."

After grabbing a change of clothes from Midnight, I turn back towards the motel, on the lookout for number ten. I scan the door numbers, some of which are hard to make out from the rusting, but quickly find my room at the sharp corner of the motel. Good thing it's a small place. I'm so tired I can barely keep my eyes open.

As I'm fumbling with the keys, a man steps out from the adjacent room. His eyes slightly widen when he sees me. I guess he's just as surprised to see another soul as I am. He is dressed smartly in jeans and a Harrington jacket over a loosely knotted tie, hanging beneath an unbuttoned shirt collar. His hair is neatly styled, and his posture suggests a mix of haste and curiosity.

"Hey, neighbor," he greets me with an unexpectedly warm voice.

"Hey," I reply, shaking his extended hand.

"It's rare to see a new face here."

"I'm just here to catch on some sleep," I say with a shrug, trying to keep it short.

"Let me guess... you're a trucker?"

I nod, offering a tired smile, hoping he gets the message.

He grins and says, "Well, I hope you get some good sleep. Look like you need it, my friend."

"This is your place?" I gesture around. Don't know why I ask, I guess my curiosity got to me.

"Oh no," he chuckles. "Just a frequent visitor... Anywho, gotta run, the local store's closing soon. It's a Sunday." His voice is deep, but there's a whimsical playfulness to it.

Seems like a decent guy. Shame I just ain't in the mood to make friends. I bid him a farewell nod and open the door to room ten. Entering the room, the first thing that catches my attention is an old, rickety desk flush against the wall. I drop my stuff down on the worn chair facing it, then collapse onto the bed, not even bothering to remove my shoes.

The room is not a pretty sight—walls painted a ghastly shade of dirty yellow and the only options for light are a lamp with a bulb so dim it's practically useless, and an overhead bulb bright enough to make the cockroaches run for cover. The bed feels like a slab of concrete, but to a man who's been cooped up in a truck cab for hours, it's a minor inconvenience compared to the luxury of space. I've stayed in my fair share of budget motels, and this isn't the worst, not even close. Each of my limbs pulls themselves in opposite directions as if I'm Stretch Armstrong. My mind dozes off for a minute, taking me to Sally and the ranch. Don't know if it's a dream or a daydream. Maybe it's something in between.

A racket outside yanks me back to the dirt-yellow room. My ears pick up two voices, a male and female. I roll over on the brick of a bed, trying to muffle the yelling with a pillow.

No luck. The sound of glass breaking shatters any thought I had of getting back to sleep, making me groan. My body forces itself up on the bed, and I rub the sleep away from my eyes, then glance at my watch—8 PM. Got about five hours of shut-eye. Need to make sure I snooze a bit more before hitting the road again. I lift myself up from the bed and peer through the curtains, spotting the culprits.

"Goddamn it!" I mutter under my breath. It's the couple from the gas station. They're loud enough to wake the dead. I crack the door open a bit to listen better. I usually mind my own business, but my curiosity has gotten the better of me. You know what they say about curiosity.

"Da hell you mean you lost it, Jed?" the woman screeches, her hair sprouting even wilder than before. She's sporting a fresh black eye that shines a hundred shades of purple beneath the streetlamp's monochrome glow.

"I didn't lose the gun, Mabel," the man shouts back. "Must've been swiped. I stashed it under the mattress!"

"Like hell!" the woman shouts again. "You're always losing our shit!"

They're staggering about, clearly plastered, pieces of a broken beer bottle crunching beneath their feet. Watching them is like a car crash—you can't look away. I shut the door softly and slump against it.

Their argument rages on, back and forth between their room and the outside, until finally, the man whoops,

"Mabel, I found it! It was in the damn fridge! What retard put it there?"

I can't help but chuckle at their idiocy. Hoping to avoid any more encounters with them, my feet carry me back to bed. They're begging to be freed from my boots, so I oblige, lining them up neatly at the foot of the bed.

3

I'm about to peel off my socks when a sudden craving for a smoke hits me. The nicotine has too much of a hold over me to be ignored, so I reluctantly grab my pack of Marlboros and slip into a pair of overused motel slippers.

Outside, the guy with neat hair and mustache is having a smoke too. I walk up to him. He pulls a smile and offers me a light, which I accept with a polite nod.

"Frosty evening, eh?" he says.

I grunt in acknowledgement. He's only trying to make polite conversation, but I can't stop from showing a tinge of annoyance, my poor mood lingering from being rudely awoken by those two clowns. I always try to be polite. I've got enough on my mind without making enemies.

"So, where's that load of yours headed?" he asks.

"Sacramento," I say, glancing at him before shifting my gaze. He seems a tad younger than me, perhaps in his late forties.

"Not a big talker, huh?" he asks, chuckling to himself. "Guess that's why you became a trucker."

"Nah, I'm beat. Been driving straight from Texas non-stop."

"My old man's from Texas. Lubbock, ever heard of it?"

"That's something," I say, my annoyance momentarily forgotten. "My wife's from Amarillo. Small world. We lived there before moving out to Fort Worth."

"The thing I miss most is this little diner in Waco. They made the best chicken fried steak."

"Oh, that place is a gem," I agree. Suddenly, a warm memory surfaces, bringing a smile to my face. "Nothing like their chicken fried steak."

The man observes my face and takes a drag of his cigarette. "Look at that, got a grin outta you in the end, didn't I?" He extends a hand, which I don't ignore. "I'm Malcolm, by the way. Sterling. Malcolm Sterling. But you can call me Mal."

"I'm Hank Griffin," I say. "Yeah, thinking about that diner brought back some good times with my wife. Might swing by Amarillo again after this job."

"Where are you and your wife set up now?"

"I'm living in El Paso these days. Sally passed about a year ago. Cancer." I say with my head hung low, taking a drag on my cigarette.

"Sorry to hear that. I didn't mean to stir up memories."

I brush it off with a wave of my hand. "It's alright, how could you know?"

"I split from my wife four years back, because things just didn't line up."

"How so?" I never normally pry, but now that we've started talking, I might as well keep the conversation going. However, he hesitates, rubbing his mustache, and I quickly realize the question has made him uncomfortable. "Never mind, none of my business."

"It's OK, Hank. I like a straight talker. Truth is, I realized I'm better off on my own."

"So, what do you do for fun? Can't imagine there's much of a single person scene around here."

"Oh, I don't know. There's plenty of fun to be found if you know where to look." He winks at me, then notices my eyes drift to the hillbilly couple's room. "You met our two friends, I assume?"

"Yeah. Did you catch the racket from that room earlier? Woke me up."

"Those damn good–for-nothings. I've seen them types around here before. Trouble through and through. Someone needs to teach them a lesson."

"I couldn't help but overhear them," I say, recalling the chaos. "Honestly, it was hard to miss all that commotion."

"Bet it was," Mal laughs. "What were they yacking on about?"

"They lost a gun, then found it," I shrug. "The whole thing was a mess."

Mal shakes his head. "Last thing they need is a gun," he says. "Unhinged, both of them."

"Damn straight. You know, I ran into them at the gas station a few miles back. Same story, arguing non-stop. Caught their eye by accident."

Mal winces. "Ouch. That's bad luck."

"The guy was itching for a fight." I say. "He was so ready to come at me."

"Probably high as kites, the pair of them," Mal says, looking at their room.

"Wouldn't doubt it," I scowl. "Their faces say it all. But now knowing that they're armed makes me uneasy."

Mal leans towards me conspiratorially and pats his waistband. "I'm strapped, don't you worry. And you're no small guy yourself, so what are you fretting about? They're just talk. Won't do shit. Can't you tell?"

"Maybe," I say. "But there's something else." I glance around, making sure we're alone. No idea why I'm talking so much with this man or why I assume he's trustworthy, but there is something about the way he carries himself and how he speaks. I never talk this much with anyone, not even over a smoke. Maybe it's the lack of sleep, or the fact that I'm on edge. No, then it hits me. The real reason I've let my guard down with this man. I'm finally willing to accept that I *need* someone to talk to.

I glance at their door and then at Mal, lowering my voice to a whisper. "Got stopped by a cop on Route 50. He told me there've been a bunch of disappearances across the state. All of them along this road."

Mal goes quiet, mulling over my words while I babble on. "Got me thinking after seeing that couple. Maybe they got something to do with it. You heard about it yourself?"

Mal doesn't reply. He suddenly looks miles away.

"You okay?" I say, giving his shoulder a gentle nudge.

"Yeah, yeah," he finally says, shuffling his feet. "Listen, I need to tell you something. Not here, though. Not with them nearby."

He's fidgeting with his hands now. What's got him so spooked?

Mal cocks an eyebrow. "You a beer guy?"

"Yeah, can't say no to a good brew," I say.

"I'll grab a couple from my room. Hang on."

I start to protest, feeling the weight of exhaustion pulling my eyelids down again. "Look, I'm really beat, I should probably—"

"Just one beer, man," he insists. "Got something important to tell you."

Something about the urgency in his voice piques my interest and, despite my tiredness, I nod my head. It's been a long time since I've had a real conversation with a real person. Perhaps not since Sally passed. Maybe it's time I made an acquaintance. I've been comfortable enough to babble about that crazy couple and the cop. So why refuse a beer with him now? I'm putting up defensive walls for no reason.

But despite all this, I am about to turn down his offer when Sally's voice pops inside my head. *Bullshit.* She's right. I *am* just bullshitting. I finally relent with a shrug, even managing a smile. "Alright, one beer."

Mal grins and heads off towards his room while I wait, smoking and enjoying a moment of solitude. The evening chill is setting in, and I regret not grabbing my jacket, but I figure this discussion will be quick.

Mal's door opens back up, his arms loaded with not two but four bottles of beer. I notice that I've been biting my nails without even realizing. Bad habit. I lower my hand and wipe my nails against the fabric of my jeans.

"Let's head to the courtyard," he says. "There's some benches."

I nod, following him to the well-kept area in the motel's center.

"What was your name, again?" Mal asks as we take a seat. "Sorry, bad memory."

I let out a subtle laugh. "It's fine," I say. "I'm Hank. Hank Griffin."

"Right, Hank." Mal pops one beer open against the other and hands it to me. "Cheers," he says, raising his bottle.

"Cheers." Our bottles clink together, and we settle down on the cold bench.

Mal takes a hearty gulp and lets out a satisfied sound. "Been a week since my last drink."

I lapse into my usual silence, sipping my beer, lost in thought while the cold night air nips at my skin.

"So, about that cop who stopped you," says Mal, breaking the silence. "He mentioned something about people going missing around here? Was he a young guy? Gelled hair, clean-shaven, around mid-thirties?"

"Yeah, that's him," I say, angling my body towards him. "You know him?"

"Sure do," Mal says. "He's one of ours."

"One of ours?"

"I'm a detective. Kept it quiet back there, in case of eavesdroppers."

I never figured he was a cop, but what do I know? Maybe this missing persons case is more serious than I thought. I take another gulp from my beer, its chill competing with the evening air.

"You're working on these missing kids, too?" I ask, suddenly seeing him in a fresh light. I don't know what to say to a detective, and I'm suddenly squirming in my seat. Is he even allowed to share information with me? Is he permitted to say that he's on this case? Perhaps he's keeping an eye on the suspicious couple, and they're suspects. Am I a suspect?

"That's right," Mal answers casually as he scratches his head. "We've been at it for three months, but it's a tough

27

nut to crack. If they're linked, then whoever is responsible is hiding their tracks real well."

I don't know whether I sound stupid, but I still want to help, so decide to offer the little I know. Speaking with a detective is far more exciting than all the fun I've had for the past year combined. "The couple back there, I saw them at the gas station. Jed and Mabel were their names. Not saying they're involved, but something's not right with them. Seem a bit off."

Mal perks up. "Jed and Mabel, huh?" he ponders, rubbing his chin. "I'll pass it up the chain. Might be worth a closer look. Could be a reward in it for you if anything comes of it. You got a good memory, huh?"

"Yeah, always been sharp. Good for puzzles and games." Curiosity piqued, I want to fire more questions at him. I don't know whether it is okay or even whether he is allowed to answer me. I conclude that he will answer if he is allowed to. "How many missing people are we talking about here?"

"Five cases on my desk," Mal says. "Could be more out there."

The conversation and the chill drive me to drink faster. I polish off my second beer, the first brews I've had in months. Suddenly, I'm itching for another, hungry for more of this rare insight into a detective's world. I glance at my watch—9 PM.

"How about one more beer?" I venture.

Mal grins. "I like the sound of that!"

After finishing the four bottles, the cold doesn't bother me anymore. We stand up and toss them into a nearby trash can before Mal excuses himself to his room to grab more beer. I'm buzzing and it's a welcome break from the usual solitude. Besides, a longer stopover won't hurt. Not when I'm ahead of schedule on my delivery.

I turn my face towards the night sky and enjoy the cold stinging my face. A few more moments pass by before I glance at my watch. By then, Malcolm's been in his room for a good five minutes now. I knock on his door but get no answer. I knock again, harder this time.

The door swings open.

"Everything okay?" I ask.

"Yes, yes, had to take a leak." Malcolm chuckles and I join him. My head is beginning to spin a little, in a good way.

Mal hands me a couple more beers and we stroll back to our bench, each lighting a fresh cigarette.

"Just keep quiet about those two for now, alright?" Mal says. "And don't mention me, especially to that young cop, if you see him again."

"Why's that?" I ask, maintaining eye contact.

"He's eager, looking to climb the ranks," Mal says. "He might poke around, blow my cover. I'll let my boss know about Jed and Mabel when the moment is right."

"Got it," I say, taking a swig of the new beer.

As we're chatting, a car rolls up—a real beater. The door groans open and a tall guy unfolds himself from the driver's seat. He hauls out a hefty hiking bag and gives us a wave on his way to reception.

"Hey there!" Malcolm calls out. I'm feeling just tipsy enough to consider making another new friend tonight, and I give him a wave with my free hand.

"Hallo," the guy responds, his accent catching me off guard. German, maybe Austrian? Definitely European, anyway.

"You're a long way from home!" Malcolm yells to him.

"I'm from Germany!" he replies, now close enough for a good look. He's tall, easily over six feet, with a blond mop of hair brushing his eyebrows, the spitting image of those guys in TV ads.

"So, what brings you to the desert?" Mal asks cheerfully.

He points to the mountains. "I'm a climber, checking off America's peaks one by one!"

We exchange glances. The motel's like a crossroads, all sorts of people passing through.

"I used to climb myself," he says. "What's your top pick?"

"Mont Blanc, without a doubt," the young German replies. "It's…" He stops to search for the right word. "Very wonderful." He pronounces the W's as V's and the V's as W's. It's kind of endearing. A lot better than my German, I suppose.

"Europe, huh?" Mal says. "Never made it out there. How about you, Hank?" He turns to look at me.

I shake my head. "Only been out of the country once."

"You don't like traveling?" the young climber asks. "The world is so big. So much to see."

I start to answer but then drift into my own thoughts. Sally had always wanted to travel the world, but I was too wrapped up in my own sense of patriotism to indulge her. Now, with her gone, traveling seems pointless. Just me and a pile of unpaid medical bills.

"He's more a traveler of the mind," Mal quips, trying to lighten the mood. I force a smile, not wanting to dampen their spirits.

"Staying at the motel tonight?" Mal asks the young hiker.

"Hope so, if there's a room," the young hiker says with a friendly grin hanging off his rosy face.

Mal sweeps his arms around the desolate place. "I'm sure there's space. Not exactly a tourist hotspot."

The German lad laughs, and I muster a half-hearted chuckle, feeling the weight of my thoughts pulling me down. I fight the urge to yawn.

"You should hit the sack," Mal says to me. "We can finish these up."

"Thanks," I say, standing up with the empty bottles. "Life on the road's got my days and nights all mixed up."

I bid Mal and the young hiker goodnight and head back to my room. Inside, I go through the motions—brushing my teeth with the half-empty amenities and washing my face. The mirror reflects a tired man with dark circles under eyes, a reminder it's nearly time for some much-needed

31

self-care. I wince at my aching gums, spitting out a trace of blood with the toothpaste. Dentists are a luxury I can't afford.

Lying in bed, I let my mind wander. Sally's voice echoes in my head. Children surround her, her playful laughter filling our kitchen. The aroma of her secret spaghetti and meatballs recipe fills the air—a family favorite. Her brothers' kids, all five of them, dart around, spreading their infectious joy. Being an uncle is the best—all the fun, none of the responsibility. But now it's just me and the silence.

As I drift off, the warmth of another memory envelops me.

Sally and I, at her eldest brother's house for a meal. Jerry, one of Sally's other brothers, strides into the kitchen, his hands gripping a bottle of whiskey that screams luxury. "Happy birthday, Hank!"

"This for me?" I ask, taking the bottle and examining the label with pursed lips.

"It's your special day!" Jerry wraps me in a bear hug. He's a navy man, more often at sea than at home in Texas. It means a lot that he's here.

"So, still trucking along?" Jerry asks.

"Yep, nearly two decades now."

"You need a break, man. I've been getting into boxing myself lately," Jerry says, throwing a few air punches. "How about a round or two sparring together sometime?"

I chuckle softly. "Never could get into boxing. Too violent for my taste."

"Shame," Jerry says. "Your old man was a real champ."

"Yeah, he was pretty damn good." I don't say it out loud, but it was boxing that made him—and boxing that ruined him, too.

"How about a hike, then?" Jerry suggests, lightening the mood.

"That, I can do," I say, gripping his shoulder and grinning.

Sally's voice chimes in from the dining room. "Dinner's ready!" The kids file towards the large dining table, packed with food, their beaming smiles light up the room.

We all gather around, savoring the moment of togetherness. All eleven of us.

4

I jolt awake in the motel room. The clock shows 23:17. No idea what woke me. Everything is quiet. I try to settle back into sleep.

Thud. My eyes flick open again. Am I still dreaming? *Thud.* The sound is like fists pounding on a table. I sit up, disoriented, trying to discern reality from dreams. A faint voice, a *woman's* voice, drifts through. I strain my ears to pick it up, but I don't hear it again. Maybe it's just the wind.

Seconds later, I hear a tiny sound again from somewhere. I try to listen closely, but can't pin down where it's coming from. The sound is not constant, so I wait, straining my ears and waiting for it to re-emerge from the silence.

I hear it again. It's extremely faint. More of a vibration than a sound. I think it's coming from below. A thought lingers that it is an animal rummaging below the floorboards. I suppose it wouldn't be unusual for a cheap motel like this to be overrun with vermin.

The sound resurfaces, this time a bit sharper. I'm certain that it's coming from below the floor. The hairs on my arms stand up. I'm not a coward, but I suppose the missing persons case has me on edge. I inch towards the floor, pressing my ear against the grimy carpet, picking up the sound once again with the same kind of vibration as before, but clearer this time. It's a metallic sound like something being moved around. Is there a basement below us?

All the things the young cop and Mal said keep haunting my mind. My heart begins to race. What if this is linked to those disappearances? I stand up, certain that I should wake Mal right away.

In a rush, I yank on my jeans and shirt. I bolt out of my room so fast that I leave the door wide open. I don't even care—there's nothing of value in there.

Seconds later, my fist pounds on Mal's door, eyes darting around, half-expecting someone to leap out of the shadows to silence me. My head is in full panic-mode, and I start to feel heart palpitations kicking in. It all seems like a thriller movie, with me being hunted down for discovering some hidden truth. I take a breath before my imagination runs away from me.

There's still no answer from Mal. I hammer on the door again, more forcefully. "Wake up, Mal!" I shout.

Finally, the door swings open, and Mal's standing there, looking half-scared. His expression changes when he sees me out of my wits. He probably thinks I've lost my mind.

"Mal, listen," I blurt out, pushing past him and rushing into the room. I don't even care about manners right now, and I'm hyperventilating. "I heard something... down below. There's gotta be a... basement or something. I heard a voice... clear as day."

"Hank, slow down, take a breath." Mal says, shutting the door. "What's going on?"

My hands are trembling. I close my eyes to calm my speeding heart rate. I'm standing here with a detective, yet my mind's racing through all the sinister possibilities. That receptionist seemed off, too aloof. Could he be involved? And that couple, they're bad news, I'm certain of it. And the foreign guy could be involved for all we know.

Mal's voice pulls me back from my thoughts. "Hank, take a seat," he says. "What you are saying sounds like you've had a nightmare. You were tired, remember? And all the talk about the disappearances must have gotten to you. I'm sorry for putting those thoughts in your head. I'm sure what you heard can be explained with the beer and lack of sleep. You were just dreaming, Hank."

"No, it wasn't a dream," I insist. "I'm sure it wasn't. I'm certain I heard noises coming from down below."

Mal reaches for a bottle of water on the nightstand. "Do you want some?" he asks.

I wave it off with a shrug, my hands still shaking. "You need to call for backup, Mal," I blurt out, immediately feeling silly for saying such words. Still, I can't stop my panic. "I know I heard something from down there. You need to check on everyone, especially that couple and the foreigner."

Mal gives me a deadpan look, clearly thinking I'm crazy, and places the water bottle back on the nightstand. "Look," he says calmly, walking up to me and putting a hand on my shoulder. "You've had a few too many, Hank. Take a deep breath."

I do as I am told, and the adrenaline subsides, yet I remain convinced I wasn't dreaming. I'm certain I heard noises. Mal watches me as I take another deep breath through the nose and exhale through the mouth. Did I really hear noises of furniture being dragged around? Or an animal? Maybe that's what my sleep deprived mind forced me to think because of the disappearances. Perhaps Mal is right, but I'm not just going to accept his reality so easily.

"Feeling better?" he asks. I nod. "If there was something going on around here, don't you think I'd hear it too?"

His words make me feel foolish. I sink into his lounge chair, my heart still pounding. "Sorry," I mumble, feeling a mix of embarrassment and confusion.

Mal walks away to pour a cup of tea from a recently boiled kettle.

"Can't sleep either?" I ask.

"Insomniac," Mal says with a tired smile. "Sleep and I aren't on speaking terms."

I chuckle weakly, accepting the tea Mal hands to me. While he's busy with his own cup, I sneak a look around his room. It's unlike mine—his bed has a softer mattress, decorated walls, and even a couple of small plants in the corner. It feels more lived-in and personal.

"You been staying here long?" I ask Mal. My eyes scan his cozy setup, and I try putting the noises I heard out of my head.

"Yeah, figured it'd be easier to just set up shop here than keep going back and forth from town." Mal said with a shrug.

"Smart," I comment, nursing my tea. But my ears reluctantly catch another faint noise. I look at Mal for a sign. He's fishing out the teabag from his cup and hasn't flinched. I guess he didn't hear it. I strain my ears and I hear the noise again. This time, I'm sure it is something to be concerned about. Wild animal or not, I know I'm not crazy. My heart pounds harder once again.

With yet another faint screech from below, my body involuntarily forces me up from the chair. "Don't tell me you can't hear that?" I ask Mal, my face creasing in alarm.

Mal looks at me as if I'm crazy. "Hear what? Hank, you might need some sleep. Sounds like the booze talking."

"No, I definitely heard something!" I say firmly, but I can see that Mal's hospitality is wearing thin.

"Let's not make a night of it," he says, reaching to take my cup.

But right then, as clear as day, I hear a rhythmic pounding coming from below our feet. I'm sure Mal can hear it too.

But when I look at his face, it remains unchanged. Am I going crazy? I don't think so. I hear the pounding once again. Instinctively, I pull out my phone and start to dial 911.

Mal's voice sharpens. "What are you doing?"

"I'm calling it in!" I shout. "Listen! How do you not hear it?"

"Put the phone away, Hank," Mal demands, his tone suddenly stern.

I press the phone to my ear, hearing the operator's faint voice, my free ear strained towards the pounding sound still carrying from somewhere below. "Nine-one-one, what's your emergency?"

Before I can speak, a searing pain explodes at the back of my head. I collapse to the floor, gasping as the room starts to spin. I reach to touch the back of my head and feel something warm on my palm. Pulling back my hand, all I now see is blood. My vision blurs. I don't know whether it is from the blow to the head or from the fear of seeing blood on my hand.

"What in the—" I struggle to speak, turning my head with great effort. Mal looms over me, a bloodied lamp in hand.

"Why?" I choke out, barely able to comprehend what's happening. *Why would he strike me on the head with a lamp? He is a detective.* Then, suddenly, my ringing head starts to put the pieces together. Mal didn't want me to

39

mention to the young cop that I'd met him. Mal knew about the disappearances. Mal pretended not to hear the noises, even when they were clear as day. I gasp at the realization.

I know I'm too late.

Mal drags me across the room, the blood smudging against the carpet.

"Didn't want it this way, Hank," he tells me. "But you've left me no choice." He rolls back a rug on the floor, revealing a hidden hatch. "But I guess now we'll have more time to chat. There's someone else I want you to meet."

My vision dims, and the world slips away into darkness.

5

My eyes slowly open up as I regain consciousness. Everything around me is a blur. The relentless throb pulsating behind my eyeballs makes me wince. Did I really drink so much last night to give me a stinking hangover? I try to raise my hand to rub my head, but I can't move. My wrists are bound to the chair. When I tug at the restraints, the knots won't loosen, but my wrists cry out in pain, the leather of the straps rubbing against them each time I twist and turn.

Not long after, I admit defeat. There's no way I'm getting out of the chair. In an attempt to regain my vision, I heavily blink several times, trying to hydrate my eye sockets. But it's freezing in here—all the blinking does is sting my eyes. A minute or so passes before my eyes can see clearly again. I'm in a tight, dimly lit space. I glance around, the back of my head throbbing even more with every move I make. The space looks like a basement. The walls are exposed brick, and the floor is bare stone. No wonder it's so damn cold.

A clanking sound of chains draws my attention to a corner of the dimly lit room, where a young woman, no older than twenty, lies shackled to the floor. Her leg is tethered to the wall by a short chain. With an awful sinking in my stomach, the realization of what's happening sets in. How can this be?

I try to speak, but my parched throat betrays me. The effort triggers a coughing fit that only intensifies the throbbing in my head.

The girl lifts her head; her face partially obscured by dirty blonde hair. "Hello," she whispers, her voice so frail I can hardly hear her as she curls into the corner.

"I'm Hank," I say, trying to ease the tension. I don't want to scare her. It looks like she's been here for some time.

"Sara," she replies, her voice still barely above a whisper.

Speaking only worsens my pain, so I study her quietly. She's wearing a miniskirt and cropped tee, both caked in dust and grime. As my eyes adjust to the light, or rather the lack of it, I notice that her right leg is covered in dry blood. She's missing a small chunk of flesh, leaving a gaping, dark wound. I start to feel nauseous and avert my gaze to a metal in the corner of the room.

"What is this place?" I ask, my voice trembling. My mouth is so dry, I can hardly speak.

"It's his basement," she murmurs, as if trying to avoid delivering terrible news. "We're below the motel."

"Whose basement?"

"Mal's."

"Mal?" I ask, still unable to accept the obvious truth lying right in front of my eyes. "But he's a detective, working undercover..."

"Guess he fooled you, too," Sara spits. Her words are laced with bitterness, but she looks defeated.

"What do you mean?" I ask, ignoring the throbbing in my head. As soon as I ask, I realize how dumb the question sounds.

"He's the motel owner," Sara replies. "Told me so himself."

"But he seemed so... so normal," I stutter. My head spins as I try to grasp the truth that I'd already begun to realize. "He knew the cop I met earlier and everything. Sounded so damn convincing."

Sara's eyes darken. "That's how he gets you." She sits up, brushing her tangled hair away from her face. "My car broke down on Route 50. He stopped, offered to help. I was desperate..." she trails off with a haunted look. I don't press her— she's been through enough.

"How long have you been here?" I ask gently.

She ponders for a moment, then says, "About a month, I think. Maybe a little less. It's hard to keep track without windows or a clock."

I muster what confidence I can, but the lack of conviction in my voice is hard to miss. "We'll get out of this, Sara. I promise." Inside, fear grabs at me. My eyes dart around the basement, desperate for an escape route. Did I at least sound a little convincing?

She points above her head. "There's no way in or out apart from that hatch there. We're not his first victims, and I don't think I'll last much longer, after what I did," she says, her voice faltering. "I don't know what's taking him so long, though."

Her words send a chill down my spine. Is she joking? Has she really been driven to the point of giving up? What's in store for me?

Sara points to her wounded leg. "This is his handiwork," she says.

Her gaze drops back to the floor. I strain against the leather straps binding me, but they're thick as hell. I eye the hatch on the ceiling, then the metal surgical cart on the other side of the room, trying to formulate the bones of a plan. A door on the far end of the basement catches my attention. "Sara, what's behind there?"

She shrugs. "I don't know. That's the place he takes them. The less fortunate ones. He disappears in there for hours with them and comes back out alone. I'm lucky he didn't take me yesterday after making such a scene. Guess he was too busy dealing with you."

"That was you making the noise? Shouting. I heard it."

"Yeah, and he made sure I regretted it," she says, her voice trailing off.

I decide not to probe further, noticing the flesh wound on her leg again. My imagination fills in the blanks.

Sara and I jump the moment the hatch above us creaks open. My heart races, fear gripping me like never before. A ladder comes down, then boots appear. Mal hums a tune as he descends, providing an eerie soundtrack to our nightmare. It's a familiar country song, but in this context, I can't place it. Nevertheless, it sends shivers down my spine. He lands on the floor with a thud, a twisted spring in his step.

"Wonderful playlist in your truck, Hank." Mal winks at me, continuing to hum. I realize it's a tune from my truck, the one that was playing as I killed the engine after pulling into the lot upstairs. What I wouldn't do to go back to that moment, then restart Midnight's big engine, and head to Sacramento. Mal starts circling me like he's playing a sordid game of musical chairs before turning his attention to Sara. She recoils, curling into a tight ball, her face buried in her arms.

"Why are you doing this?" I ask, my voice breaking. It halts Mal in his tracks, even with no real authority in it.

"I had no plan to bring you down here, Hank," Mal says, turning to me. "It never even crossed my mind. I like you, I really do. But I couldn't have police snooping around. If you want to blame someone, blame Sara here. If it wasn't for her, you would be back on the road by now."

He trunks back to look at Sara with a smile. It widens as he leers at her wound, his tongue flicking over his lip. His smile, which seemed friendly earlier, now looks grotesque and I flinch.

"But what a delightful surprise!" Mal says in a cheery voice. "Two guests at once! This is such a new experience to me!" He pauses, pondering with a finger on his lips. "I'll need to prepare a place for you to sleep," he says finally, looking at me. "But first, let's tend to that head wound."

He approaches me, unzipping a pouch slung over his shoulder. "Remember, Hank, you brought that on yourself," he says. "You should've listened to me."

I curse out and pull against my restraints. "You're going to regret this."

Mal doesn't react. He takes out bandages and cleansing wipes from the pouch and places them on the tray. "Let's get you cleaned up," he says to me, reaching out to touch my head. "Don't want an infection now, do we?"

"Don't touch me!" I grit out through my clenched teeth, defiance flickering within me. But at least if he means to fix me up, he's not about to murder me. At least not just yet.

"Now, now, no need for that," Mal chides. "I'm helping you. You should be grateful."

"Grateful?" I scoff. "You're out of your mind." I feel anger boiling over me but I am helpless, and it only worsens the pain in my head.

Mal's laughter creeps me out. "Sara was a feisty one too when she first came," he chuckles. "But don't push it, Hank. I wouldn't want to silence you permanently." The warning is clear and Sara's fearful glance reinforces it.

As Mal applies the cold wipes to the wound on the back of my head, I stifle a groan, biting down hard to keep myself from showing pain. I don't want to give him the satisfaction. My gaze drifts to the mysterious door, my mind racing with what horrors it might conceal.

"You'll need stitches," Mal says casually, as if discussing the weather. "But don't worry, I've read up on this. We'll patch you up just fine."

I glare at him, my head pounding and heart racing. "You just read up on how to stitch up a wound? What, am I your lab rat?"

"Relax, Hank," Mal says. "If you behave, we might even share another couple of nice cold beers. You're better company than that clueless reception kid."

"He's part of this sick game, too?" I ask in shock.

Mal chuckles coldly. "Him?" he retorts. "No chance. I chose the most clueless guy possible as receptionist. He's so out of it, didn't even blink when I drove your truck. Gave him a wave just to prove it to myself. Think he's zonked on OxyContin or whatever."

I can't help but spit out, "You're out of your mind."

"Now, now, Hank," Mal says, shaking his head. "Let's stay friendly, alright? I enjoy our time together. Don't ruin

47

this." His tone is eerily calm, almost mocking. This is a completely different person to whom I was speaking to earlier in the night. I grind my teeth, holding back a torrent of threats. I know it won't do any good to show.

As if reading my mind, Mal presses on my wound, forcing out a scream from me. "Let's stay civil, shall we?" he murmurs as he cleans and tightly wraps my head with bandages, each turn making me feel more trapped.

He goes round about a dozen times. "All set. Good as new! Well, nearly." His laugh is maniacal, chilling to the bone. "I didn't expect such a lively morning."

I watch him walk away. He puts away the pouch and wipes his hands against his trousers. I feel sick to my stomach, seeing him swanning around the basement, wearing that sick grin on his face.

"Well, it's time for me to head out!" Mal announces to the room. "I'll bring breakfast for my guests later."

He walks to the stepladder and turns back to look at me. "We'll sort your head out then too, Hank," he says to me in an almost fatherly manner. I feel disgusted by it. "In the meantime, just make yourself at home!"

He chuckles and climbs up the ladder. I watch as his boots disappear up to his room above us. Watching him leave, a surge of desperation grips me. With him gone, I'll be given time to think, plan something, anything. He drags the ladder back up and the hatch closes with a thud. Then I hear his heavy footsteps step further and further away. I finally let out a breath I was holding and allow my gritted teeth to relax. My head is still spinning from all the pain and the rough bandaging procedure Mal just performed on me.

"Sara," I whisper urgently.

"Yeah?" her voice is frail, barely there.

"We can't let this be the end of the line. We must try to escape this place."

"If you've got some kind of plan, I'm all ears," Sara says, biting her nails. "But I can't risk more of his punishments."

"Can you stand up and try something for me?" I ask her.

With a heavy sigh, Sara gets to her feet, adjusting her skirt discreetly. Her movements are shaky, and her fingers fidget non-stop.

"Now, see if you can reach my restraints," I tell her.

She inches forward, but the chain pulls her sharply back.

"Come on, try to get to me," I urge, but the realization slams me in the gut—the chain is too short.

Sara's arm stretches out with her fingers curled in. I can tell that she's scared.

"Easy now, I'm not gonna hurt you," I say, trying to sound as calm as I can.

Sara's hand reaches out as far as it can, stopping frustratingly short, about thirty centimeters from mine.

"Damn it!" I mutter, my escape plan vanishing into dust.

"What exactly was your plan?"

"I figured if you could just loosen one strap, I'd do the rest," I say, allowing defeat to creep into my voice. "Then get us both out of this mess somehow."

"Yeah, but how?" Sara presses. "Even if you can free yourself, there is no way out of here except the hatch."

"Does Mal lock it?" I ask. But I already know the answer.

Sara scoffs, "What do you think? And even if he doesn't lock it, I can't reach you, anyway."

Despite Mal's amateur nursing attempts, my head's still throbbing, but I try to ignore it and think as deeply as I can manage. "We need something sharp and long," I say. "Maybe an object from that cart. A scalpel, or something to cut these straps."

However, Sara has already retreated to her corner and is lying down with her back to me. I sense Mal's terror has worn her down. In desperation, I pull against the restraints, using all my strength, but it's useless. I'm just exhausting myself further.

Sara speaks from her corner, still facing the wall. Her voice drops to a whisper of resignation. "Like I said before, it won't matter even if you get yourself free. The hatch closes from the outside. You won't be able to open it. He even took this chain off my leg after the second week. He knows I wouldn't be able to escape, and he only shackled me again to punish me."

I stop struggling in my chair. I suppose it's no use. Might as well preserve my strength. "Sara, where were you headed before... all this?" I ask, trying to keep the conversation going. I want to keep some sliver of hope alive, burning inside her. And me.

Sara doesn't immediately respond. I wonder if she's given up completely now. I think about repeating the question, but then she whispers to me.

"California. I wanted to be closer to my boyfriend." Then, almost as an afterthought, she adds, "What about you?"

"I'm just a truck driver. Was on my way to a delivery. Clothes for some company called Deranga."

Sara's eyes show a flicker of light. "Oh, I know that brand. Love their stuff, even if it is too expensive for my purse."

"I'll make sure you get your pick when we're out of here," I assure her with a half-hearted chuckle, trying to lift her spirits. "Just between us, okay?"

For the first time since I woke up inside the gloomy basement, I see the corners of Sara's mouth lift to reveal a small smile. I feel like I've achieved a small victory. Now that I think about it, she reminds me of our daughter, Olivia. She had those same expressive eyes and arched eyebrows that always gave away what she was feeling. She would have grown into a beautiful woman, just like Sara.

We lapse into silence again. Time creeps by, the silence only being broken by our shared breaths and the sound of water dripping from a tap on the other side of the room. Eventually, nature calls to me.

"Uh, Sara, I need to use the bathroom," I say. My eyes dart helplessly around the room, the absurdity of my situation sinking in. I know I'm helpless, strapped to this chair.

"There's no bathroom. Mal gave me that bucket." She nods towards a dingy blue bucket near her feet. "I empty it into the drain by the shower afterwards." She says it like it's the most normal thing in the world. I guess she's far past the point of humiliation.

I curse under my breath, turning my eyes away from the bucket.

As desperation kicks in once more, my body twists and turns in the chair, but I soon realize it's another futile attempt. Ten minutes go by while I sit and squirm, then ten more. I can't take it anymore.

"Mal!" I yell at the top of lungs. It makes my need to pee even more unbearable. My waterworks aren't as tip top as they used to be, and when the urge comes on strong, it comes real quick. "I need to use the bloody bathroom! Now!"

Sara's reaction to my shouting is instant. She shoots up from the spot where she is lying down and begs me to stop. "Please, Hank. Please, don't do this." I see absolute fear in her eyes when she looks up at the closed hatch, and her voice trembles. "He'll hear you!"

"That's the point!" I say impatiently. "Hey, Mal!" I shout again, my voice echoing off the cold walls.

"No, please!" Sara pleads. She is constantly looking at the hatch, then back at me again, scared for her life.

"He gets furious when we make noise!" she says. "We can't anger him again!"

I feel sorry for the poor girl. I can't imagine the horrors she's gone through during the time she's been here. I don't want her to be scared, but I can't be tied down to this chair any longer, either. Something Sara said earlier pops to my head. When I first opened my eyes, she said that Mal will get rid of her now that I was here.

"I'll take the heat," I say to her reassuringly. "It's me he'll come after. I'm the one who shouted." Though a part of me wonders whether I'm ready for what Mal might do.

Sara is shaking, tears streaking down her face. "You don't understand, Hank!" she cries. "You don't know what a monster he is. He'll punish us both. Please, don't provoke him. I don't want him to... do what he did last time. I can't take it again."

Then it dawns on me as clear as daylight—my life is not the only one I should be worried about. There's another soul in this room, one with an actual future beyond these walls. I can't be reckless, not with her life at stake. I guess being alone for so long after Sally's death, I'm not used to thinking about anyone but myself. Now, the situation is different. I'm not a truck driver anymore. I am a prisoner, trapped in a sadist's basement, with only another victim for company. A young girl, for that matter. I need to be more

53

cautious. Can't have anything happen to her just because of my stubbornness. Worse, I won't be able to live with myself if I witness Mal doing something to a helpless girl. I picture him upstairs, getting on with his day. Can't believe he's the same guy I shared drinks with just yesterday. Is this the punishment for breaking my streak of avoiding company?

The ominous sound of footsteps echoes above us, each step a heavy beat getting closer to the hatch. The fear in Sara's eyes transforms into full-blown terror. However, in a fleeting moment of hope, I envision a rescue.

The hatch swings open, revealing a blinding beam of flashlights. My eyes adjust to see the young cop whom I had met earlier, descending a rope ladder with a flashlight between his teeth.

I throw myself at his mercy and thank him.

"You're safe now," the cop assures us, helping Sara up.

But the harsh reality crashes back. There is no rescue. Not now and maybe never.

"Hank!" Mal's familiar, menacing voice snaps me back to reality. He looms over me, his face twisted in irritation. His fist connects unexpectedly with my jaw. The suddenness of the blow sends pain shooting through my neck and the back of my head. The pain which had gone numb starts to throb and ring again.

"You couldn't keep him quiet, could you?" Mal's tone is eerily jovial as he turns to Sara. as if scolding mischievous children.

He turns back to me. "What's your problem, Hank?" he asks me. "Am I not being a good host to you?" he leers in my face. I've never wanted to wrap my hands around someone's throat and throttle the life from them before, but right now I want to hurt Mal so badly I can taste it.

"I need to use the bathroom," I hiss through gritted teeth, holding back my rush of anger and disgust.

Mal pauses, as if pondering a puzzle. "Tricky with you all tied up, eh?"

He then glances around, almost theatrically, shrugging his shoulders as if performing a mime.

My gaze shifts to Sara, who is lying still in her corner. It's obvious she is scared out of her wits, perhaps trying her best to melt into the background, thinking she can remain invisible to him. But Mal moves towards her, reaching out his hand.

My stomach churns. Before I can stop myself, I blurt out, "Mal, leave her alone."

He ignores me. His hand lands on Sara's shoulder, caressing her, then giving her arm a soft squeeze. My gaze scatters, a mix of disgust and helplessness washing over me. I desperately struggle against my restraints, but I know the attempt is futile.

"I'm warning you, Mal. Get the hell off her."

Mal snaps to face me. "Or what, Hank? What the fuck are you going to do, huh?"

Sara starts whimpering, and I desperately want to cover my ears. My eyes close tight, not wanting to see what is about to unfold. But Sara's whimpers suddenly stop and my eyes snap back open. She's curled herself back into a ball, but Mal's walking towards me.

"Let's sort you out, Hank," Mal says, clasping a bucket in one of his hands. "Clearly, your need for a piss is making you cranky. I guess a guy your age hasn't got the prostate he used to. I shouldn't be such a bad host."

He places the bucket on the floor, then bends down. My body tenses up. *What is he doing? Is he going to untie my hands?* I think about various ways to attack him. With my head perhaps, or maybe strangling him would be better. Although I'm not sure whether my hands are strong enough to do that. They've been tied up for some time now, and they've gone numb from the lack of blood flow. My grip might be as weak as a child's. Except I know what adrenaline can do. I'm guessing if I smash my head against the bridge of his nose hard enough, he'll drop, giving us a chance to escape. More solutions run through my mind in the split second Mal bends down.

When his hands extend towards my groin, I realize his true intentions and my face contorts into a disgusted frown as Mal undoes my belt and releases the top button of my pants.

"What the fuck are you doing?" I try to wriggle myself away from his meddling hands.

"Don't flatter yourself, Hank," Mal laughs as he unzips me. "Would you prefer I let you piss your pants like a little boy?"

"Don't you dare touch me!" Even to my own ears, I sound weak and defeated. Mal ignores my feeble warning and continues.

He places the bucket against my thighs, then grabs a firm hold of my junk and points it towards the bucket. I grit my teeth in disgust. Anger, frustration and embarrassment—all are there, tangling up inside me in a weird way that I have never experienced before. Or at least not in decades. Shame washes over me like a wave. Shame like when my grandma caught me with a kid from the neighborhood, pants down, comparing our boy parts, and she hauled the kid's parents over to tell them what we'd been doing.

"Come on, Hank," Mal orders. "I've got better things to do than hold your old Johnson in my hands. Want me to whistle?"

What choice do I have? Mal looks at my face with a sneer, so I shut my eyes. It takes me a while, but I finally manage to get going. The sound of liquid hitting the bucket reaches my ears, and after opening my eyes, I see some has splashed onto Mal's hands and on my jeans. I feel sick to my stomach. It just adds to the indignity. Mal acts as if it's nothing; like he's glad to be doing me a favor. I get a strong whiff of the piss as its unhealthy stench fills the room.

"Good boy, Hank," he says with a smirk as he puts the bucket away and zips me up, then follows it up with a pat on my head in a patronizing manner. "Although judging from the color, you might be a little dehydrated. Make sure to drink some water."

Mal strolls away to empty the bucket into the drain by the water tap that Sara called a shower. I watch him sniff the air with a weird satisfaction. My nose wrinkles in response. When I turn towards Sara, it appears she's not moved an inch.

Strategies are forming in my head. I must keep on Mal's good side where possible. He's clearly fucked in the head—if I can just get him to believe that I won't try anything, maybe he'll let his guard down, and that's when I'll have my chance to overpower him. But the longer I wait, the more likely it is that he'll realize I'm of no value to him, and decide to dispose of me.

"Better now?" Mal asks, looking around all smug after putting the bucket down. "No more complaints?"

I stare at him blankly, unsure what to think or say at the absurdity of this whole situation. Without a bladder full of pee pressing against my parts, I can think better. Yes, I need to play the good little captive.

"Thanks, Mal. Feel much better now."

"Well, I guess that is it," Mal says with a slight nod of acknowledgement. He rubs his palms together and walks towards the ladder, but stops and turns towards us once more. "I need to get going. Be on your best behavior, understood? Any more noise from either of you and I think we may just have to break up this little party. Much fun as it is, ain't worth the risk."

Sara's head snaps up at the rough tone. She nods repeatedly like a robot, while my head hangs down low. Pretending to be thankful to this bastard has sucked away a piece of my soul. His warning is reeling through my mind. I'm afraid to admit it, but I'm terrified. For the first time in my life, whether I live or die is entirely in the hands of another person. An unhinged maniac. I've never felt so powerless in my life.

Mal climbs up the ladder and shuts the door of the hatch, locking us inside once more. The room goes silent after his footsteps fade away, but the smell from my urine lingers.

"Sorry 'bout that," I say to Sara, my voice a rough whisper.

"For what?" she asks, sounding puzzled.

"The smell. Mal was right. Wasn't the healthiest pee in the world."

She sighs. "Guess I've gotten used to it," she says. "Don't worry about it."

I'm silent for a moment. The humiliation has knocked the defiance right out of me.

"Well, sorry, anyway."

"Don't let it eat at you," Sara advises. "Mal's... easier to deal with if you don't fight back."

"He's out of his damn mind," I state, bitterness creeping into my voice.

"Yeah, I know, but that's how I've lasted," Sara says. "There were others before me. They weren't as cooperative."

"Others? Where are they now?" I ask, with a sense of dread building inside me again, quickly replacing the humiliation.

Sara's eyes flick to the shut door. "Through there," she says. "Once they go in, they never come back. Just screams, then nothing. Mal returns alone, all smiles and covered in blood. You can figure out the rest."

A chill runs across my body as I look towards the door, my mind racing with gruesome thoughts about the horrors that must've taken place behind there. The prospect of what Mal does to these people is enough to make my blood run cold.

And the likelihood is I'll find out for myself one day. One day soon, if I don't figure out how to keep Mal happy.

Sara's got this far-off look as she tells me about her first days here. "Mal was something else when I got here. Had me in that chair like a specimen for his sick games." She pauses for a second before continuing. "He... he started biting into me. Frequently. That's how I got this wound." She points towards the blackened scab on her leg. "But I talked him round, told him he'd get lonely without me.

Guess it made something click in him. I think that's why he's still keeping me alive."

"Well, whatever you did, it worked," I say, still trying to wrap my head around Mal's twisted mentality.

"Yeah, I figured he was starved for affection or something," Sara says. "His twisted idea of love's a whole other level of messed up. He doesn't just love with his heart. He's all about the flesh and blood." She pauses and I see her shudder.

"Hank, whatever you do, stay on his good side. I overheard you two yesterday. Thought you'd bring help, but Mal's too good at playing folks for fools. He's like a puppet master with his toys."

"Don't give up just yet," I tell her, trying to sound more convinced than I feel. "A cop pulled me over on the road when I came through a few miles back from here. They know people are going missing around Route 50. They'll find my truck abandoned and they'll start asking questions about whether it's linked to the others. And then they'll come looking. Don't you worry,"

Sara lets out a sad laugh. "I wish I could believe that. You haven't seen what I've seen. People come and none of them ever leave here."

Her words hit me hard. For a moment, I can't speak. What can you even say to something like that?

"You were heading to LA, right?" I ask, shifting gears, trying to occupy my racing thoughts with something—anything.

"Yeah, LA," she answers, perhaps a trace of distant dreams in her voice.

"Have you been there before?" I ask.

She shakes her head. "Nope, but I've always wanted to," she says. "Beaches, Sunset Strip, you know.... I was gonna check out some clubs and see Taylor Swift live. But, well..."

"Taylor Swift?" I ask, feeling out of the loop. "Is she real famous? Can't say I know the name."

"You don't know Taylor Swift?" Sara asks as though I'm living in the stone age. Perhaps I was. Well, I sure am now. There's a trace of amusement on her face. Seeing her smile, even only a little, warms my heart. "She's only, like, the biggest pop star alive."

I shrug. "That's not really me. I'm more about country and western. Nobody's bigger than Merle Haggard and Willie Nelson in my world. Not even your Taylor Smith."

"Taylor Swift, silly," Sara says with a girlish giggle before shooting me this look, like she's not buying it. "You sure you're not playing with me? You genuinely haven't heard of her?"

I shake my head. "Scouts honor. Have you heard of Merle Haggard?"

"No, sorry."

"Damn. I guess you haven't heard the good stuff then," I tell her. "Real country music's something else."

"Then sing me something." Sara wrinkles her nose, challenging me with a faint smile tracing her lips. "Show me what it's really like."

I'm a bit thrown off. "Sing for you?" I stutter.

"Yeah, why not?" she asks. "I could use a real distraction down here, and what better than music?"

I hesitate, trying to shake off the growing awkwardness. "I've only ever sung for my wife. And to Midnight, of course."

"Midnight?"

"My truck," I say with a faint grin on my face as well. For a moment, both me and Sara are actually talking like two normal people and not two of a sadist kidnapper. After the recent embarrassment, this conversation is helping me forget my shame, making me feel like a human being once more. After all, Sara has been here longer than me and has endured this for God-knows-how-long. I feel sorry for her and proud at the same time. She is one tough girl to survive this long.

"Well, that's one lucky truck," Sara says, the faint smile still playing on her lips. "But come on, Hank, I could really use a song."

She is right. We both could use some cheer. She deserves it, although it might be further punishment. To her ears, anyway. "Alright, just one song," I say.

Sara nods eagerly, sitting cross-legged on the floor. The difference in her expression is instant. When Mal was here, it was the face of a scared rabbit, but now it looks like the face of an enthusiastic little kid waiting for a candy bar.

As Sara adjusts her position on the floor, I begin singing a classic tune, one about getting through tough times. How apt. My voice is rusty, but I try my best to do the song justice without being too loud. Soon, I'm lost in the words of the song, my eyes scrunched shut.

When I finish, Sara lets out a little ripple of applause and says, "That was beautiful."

"Ah, it's nothing much," I say with a shrug, sensing my face flushing. "My voice ain't what it used to be."

"No, really, it was nice," Sara insists. "You have a good voice, Hank."

I can't help but feel a tiny stab of awkwardness from the praise, although I appreciate her kind words. When we eventually loop back to silence, I quickly get lost and drift deep into my thoughts, until I awaken on the porch of my home, sitting beside Sally. Sun's shining bright, and Olivia's running around in the front yard, chasing butterflies.

"What a gift," says Sally. "Aren't we just lucky, Hank?

I give her a nod. "We sure are. How's she doing at school?"

"Good, got her school report back just yesterday. All the teachers love her, and her grades are coming on."

"Luckiest parents in the world. She's smart *and* she's pretty."

Sally leans in closer. "And, she says she's got a boyfriend."

"Boyfriend?" I say, nearly spitting out my iced tea. "She's fourteen, dammit."

"Don't you worry, Hank, it's quite innocent between them. Had lunch with his mom last week—wonderful woman. A good Christian, too. He's been raised right, so you don't need to be worried about..." Sally's voice lowers. "About you know what."

"Damn right I shouldn't be worried about you know what at her age. And if I get cause to think otherwise, this young man won't touch the ground."

"When's your next job?"

"I'm back on the road next Tuesday. But I'll only be gone for three days, so don't worry. I'll be back before you know it."

"I'll miss you. Hate it when you go away."

"I'll miss you too. But it pays well."

A sigh escapes Sally's lips. "That's the only reason I let you do it. I was thinking, maybe I should look for a new job myself. Might take the pressure off you, Hank. Being a florist doesn't pay so good."

I reach out and place my hand on hers. "I know how much you love working there. Don't even think about giving it up for a few extra dollars. If we need more money, I can take on extra work."

"I'm just thinking, Olivia may only be fourteen now, but in a few years, she'll already be off to college, and we don't have any money saved."

"Don't worry, I'll take care of it, I promise."

Sally gives me a warm smile. She was always the one thinking about the future, whereas I only worried about the next twenty-four hours, and barely even that. She was the glue holding our family together through all the ups and downs.

"Oh, Hank. Come look," she says enthusiastically, pulling me into the yard. "I planted some new plants today."

I follow her through the lush grass. Both sides of the picket fence are adorned with beautiful plants—marigolds, crocuses, daffodils. We have it all. The cool wind blows in my direction, carrying the aromas along with it, and it hits me how lucky I am. Sally would even make a habit of calling me during her lunch breaks, aware of the crushing loneliness that came with the territory. The life of a long-distance truck driver.

"Here," says Sally, kneeling down by a bed of lilies, tenderly brushing her fingers against the velvety petals. "Aren't they just beautiful, Hank?"

"Yes, they are."

I look back towards Olivia. She runs towards me and jumps up to give me a hug.

"I love you, Dad."

"Love you too, sweetheart."

6

Sara and I are lost in conversation, going back and forth on various things that were happening in our lives. Well, I'll admit it's mostly her doing the talking. I probably bored her to death, speaking about Midnight for a full twenty minutes before realizing I don't have much else to spout about.

"So, what do you do aside from driving your truck? Are you married?"

"Used to be."

Sara leans forward, her eyebrows raised. "Divorced?"

"Widowed." I try not to sound too down, but the reminder of her being gone revives the wretched feeling of when she passed.

"Oh, I'm sorry." Sara's expressive eyes widen. They understand my pain.

"Shit happens, and life goes on, I guess." I hope she drops the subject, otherwise she'll end up finding out about my daughter too—I don't want to see her sob her eyes out on my behalf. "Anyway, how about you? Your folks still living up in South Carolina?"

"They're divorced. Momma took the house as part of the settlement. Dad, I think still lives somewhere in the state too, but I don't see him."

"Sorry to hear that."

"Don't be. Dad's a real piece of work. I cut him off as soon as I turned eighteen. Moved as far away as possible. Let's just say he wasn't very nice to either of us."

I connect the dots, feeling sorry for her. My own father, the boxer, was certainly no lovable patriarch. He was strict, with the word discipline at the top of his dictionary, but one thing he never did was lay a finger on me. Guess he left all his rage in the ring.

"I still speak with momma from time to time, but it's not the same anymore. I think she blames herself too much for not splitting from him sooner. And it's almost funny how just as I finally got my freedom, I've been trapped again."

"Well, when we get out of here, you should go see her. I'm sure you'll feel differently after... after all this. Being put through such an ordeal tends to shift your perspective." I look around the cold, empty basement, in the vain hope that some ideas might come to me. "So, the only way out is the hatch?"

"Yeah, I think so. But I don't know what's on the other side of that door." She points towards the other side of the

69

basement, towards the other door, hiding God knows what awful secrets.

"And he keeps the door locked at all times?"

Sara nods. "He always has the key with him. Never seen him without it."

I chew my lips. They're sore and cracked. "Do you think I would be able to kick it open?"

She shakes her head. "Don't think so. From the sound it makes when it bangs shut, it's real heavy."

Armed with this new information, I stare at the door. I think it's like the ones used in freezer rooms. Probably made of reinforced metal. Seen enough of those in my time from when I used to haul beef carcasses years back.

"I see..." I look back up to the hatch. "Well, if we were to move the chair or that table, we'd be able to reach the hatch. I'm sure if we tried hard enough, we could break through it. We'd just need Mal to trust us enough to leave us unchained."

"But what if Mal's in his room? He'll hear us and punish us."

"Then we'll need to be sure we do it when we're sure he's not in the room. He must leave this place sometimes. We'll strike when he goes out to the shops, or leaves on whatever errands he runs."

"Okay, we can try," she says, her voice quivering. She does not sound convinced. I know she's scared. I'm afraid too, but we don't have much time. Sooner or later, Mal will grow bored with us, and it will be our turn to die. Our turn to take a trip beyond that metal door and see what awfulness awaits on the other side. And there's no knowing when that might be.

"What about a back-up plan?" she says. "In case... we run out of time?"

"Well, if he decides it's the end of the line for us, all we can do is fight. If I wasn't tied to this damn chair, maybe I could overpower him."

"And if he has a knife?"

"Then I'll have to just hope luck is on my side. What have we got to lose, anyway? Maybe you can go behind him, hit him with over the head with something heavy." I look around. "The shower head, that ought to do it. There's not really anything else here we can use. For both ideas, we need to be free. I won't have any luck tied down to this chair, so I guess I'll need to convince him I'm not a threat. I mean, until I arrived, you weren't chained up, right?"

"After a while, he just left me unshackled. I was obedient enough that he didn't see me as an escape threat anymore. But you're bigger and stronger."

"And uglier, too," I say, trying to lighten the mood. "Well, it's not a great plan but better than no plan at all. Gain his trust and wait until he lets his guard down. Then, we strike."

Both of us jump in our skins when we hear the hatch creak open. We were so lost in conversation that I almost forgot about being Mal's prisoner. The cheeriness present between us seconds ago vanishes in a cold instant.

A big backpack and several cardboard boxes fall onto the basement floor through the hatch. The ladder follows, and Mal's boots clomp down the bouncy rungs soon after. Sara curls back into her ball and begins quietly humming a tune, her arms protecting her face as if she doesn't want to see him. I still can't imagine what horrible things she has gone through to be this way. My blood boils when Mal finally steps into the basement, looking smug.

"Look who's playing Santa today!" he says with a twisted cheerfulness, gesturing towards the backpack and the boxes on the floor.

Sara straightens up and pushes her skirt down, like she's bracing herself. I suppose she's got this act down to a fine art. Mal turns to me with a smile on his face. My entire body tenses in response.

"Hank, a man's company is new for us down here," he says, with a weird kind of sincerity in his voice. "I want you to be comfortable. I say that as a friend."

I decide to act upon Sara's advice from earlier, even though I have to fight back the bile rising in my throat. "Thanks, Mal," I say through gritted teeth.

"How's the head?" he asks me, his face creasing with concern. "And the jaw?" I can't tell whether the sympathy is sincere or pure mockery. The guy must be one hell of a Texas Hold 'Em player.

"Head's still numb," I say. "Jaw's fine."

Mal nods with a chuckle and starts unpacking. First thing he pulls out is this thin mattress. It is more like a quilt, really. He lays it near Sara, who flinches when he draws close.

"Your new bed, Hank," Mal says to me. "I got a great deal on it!"

"Thanks," I mutter. "But I'd be more grateful if I can take a leak without an audience."

"Oh, don't worry, Hank," Mal laughs. "I'm not going to babysit you forever. Got my own life to lead, you know."

I just nod, but inside my brain is screaming. *If I wasn't restrained right now, I wouldn't hesitate to bash your head in, Mal, you bastard. You may be laughing now, but once I get a chance, you'll be the one begging for your life.*

"I've got more stuff for you both!" Mal says like he's announcing the winners of a lottery draw. He pulls out some pieces of clothes from the backpack. "Look, I've got new clothes from the thrift shop! I picked out what I thought you'd like. Had to estimate your sizes. Wasn't that thoughtful of me?"

He then pulls out a drill from the backpack and sets it down with a smile that sends shivers down my spine. He also takes out a long, thick chain and a handful of nails.

"Time for some renovation!" he announces. I force a smile that I hope conveys gratitude, but inside, I'm anything but thankful. No, I can only imagine the drill spiraling into my exposed flesh, splintering bone, the awful sound it might make like cracking a wishbone on Thanksgiving.

Mal looks up as if he suddenly remembers something. "Oh, need some tunes for this," he says, and quickly scrambles up the ladder. A few minutes pass before he returns with a radio, turning it on immediately. The heavy thud of rock music fills the basement, drowning out every sound. It's so loud and aggressive that it blocks out even my thoughts. How can people listen to this noise?

Mal gets right to work, drilling holes in the wall almost at random. The drill bites into the brick, scattering dust and debris. The dust cloud makes its way to Sara, sending her into a coughing fit. She scoots away as much as her chain allows her to.

"You okay, sunshine?" Mal asks her as he stops the drill. His tone is unnervingly gentle.

"Yes, Daddy," Sara replies, her voice small and eyes wide. They are full of terror and on the verge of tears. "Just a tickle in my throat from the dust."

Mal puts the drill down and strokes her hair. She doesn't react, just stays still like a statue. It's clear she's used to this routine.

"You're such a good girl," Mal murmurs to her. "Not like the others. I love you."

"I love you too, Daddy." She's like a child's doll, at the mercy of her owner. *Look, kids, she even pisses herself and cries when she's hungry.*

Hearing the exchange makes my stomach churn, but I manage to hold a straight face. Remember Sara's advice—play his game, become part of his twisted world. It's the only way to survive. Wait for the right moment to strike...

Mal resumes his work, securing a heavy clasp to the wall and attaching a new, longer chain to it.

"Look at that," he says finally, stepping back to admire his handiwork. "Nice and neat, huh?"

"Looks great," I manage to blurt out, although every word feels forced. "You sure know your way around a drill."

"Now, let's get you sorted," Mal says, wading towards me through the dust. He pulls out a large syringe filled with some clear liquid. My heart begins to race.

"Seventy milligrams," Mal says. "Same as what I gave Sara last time. You're bigger, of course, but don't want to take chances with your wellbeing, do I?"

The sudden turn of events has pushed my ability to play along to the limit. I have to fight against my instinct to squirm and scream and do anything to avoid his needle. Instead, I hold still, like a good little boy receiving his medicine.

Sara avoids my gaze, looking down. The needle pricks my arm, the liquid cold as it enters my bloodstream. "You'll feel sleepy soon," Mal tells me gently. "Don't fight it. You'll wake up good as new."

I watch him place the syringe down. He then starts sweeping the dust and brick bits to the side. "Might as well make use of you, so I'll leave you a brush to clean this up," he says casually, and then just stands there, hands hanging by his sides, watching me. At least that means he doesn't intend for me to die. Not yet. But he's no more of an anesthesiologist than I am a NASCAR driver.

Minutes drag on. I feel my eyelids grow heavy and my heartbeat slows. My body relaxes despite my mind screaming to stay alert, and my thoughts stretch out and fade. I close my eyes and hear Mal's footsteps approaching closer and closer.

"Hank, you asleep?" Mal whispers, snapping his fingers near my ear. I don't give him a sign, staying perfectly still.

Mal's voice is laced with a sick excitement. "Let's get started!" I hear him rummaging around the cart, then feel the sharp prick of another injection at the back of my head. Must be another anesthetic, but I wonder why he'd bother if I'm supposed to be out cold. Fear tries to kick back in, but my mind's teetering on the edge of consciousness. Blessed relief. One moment, I'm catching the sounds of the basement. The next, I'm drifting, thinking of Midnight, my little house back home, and Sally in her rocking chair.

Reality snaps back with a jolt as a needle pierces my scalp. I can feel Mal sewing the wound at the back of my head, a dull, throbbing pain with each stitch. It's just enough to keep me on edge, but I dare not let on that I'm awake. At least it means he's not about to start sawing me into pieces.

The whole ordeal drags on, feeling like an eternity. I'm fading in and out, my body occasionally twitching, which Mal chalks up to dreaming. I keep my eyes shut tight. It's a terrible feeling, not quite being awake but not being totally under, with at least part of my mind able to comprehend what is happening. It's like sleep paralysis.

Then Mal says something to Sara, his voice almost affectionate. "I hope you like him as much as I do. Can't bring myself to do him in. Just doesn't sit right with me, y'know?"

I'm not sure if Sara responds or if I lose consciousness again. He may be keeping me alive for now, for his own entertainment. But given everything Sara has said, eventually I will be next in line to meet our creator. I didn't think to ask her just how many others there were before us, but if he had the heart to kill his other victims, what chance do we have, really? The more I wait, the less time I'll have to act. Not just for my sake, but for Sara's, too. She's too young to be another statistic. I know this now—I'd gladly give my life for hers.

When Mal ties off the final stitch, I hear his self-satisfied declaration. "Voila! Not too shabby, huh?" he exclaims. "Maybe I missed my calling as a surgeon!" His laugh is chilling.

There's a brief silence, then he calls out to Sara. "Sara, you okay? You look a little pale."

"I'm fine, Daddy," Sara's voice suggests she's playing the part well. "I just don't like the sight of blood much, you know? Makes me feel sick."

"Oh, sweetheart, I'll clean this up soon," Mal reassures her.

I hear the chains rattling as he frees Sara. "You can move around now. Just remember this: behave or it's back in chains."

"I'll be good," Sara assures him, her voice small and submissive.

I feel Mal's cold hands on me, unclasping my restraints. My heart beats double-time. A thousand thoughts rush through my head. If I play dead, he'll just chain me up like he did Sara, and who knows when we'll have another chance of springing our escape plan. This is the moment I was waiting for. It may not be the exact plan we agreed on, but this might be our only shot, especially while the hatch is open and I'm not restrained. Beggars can't be choosers, and right now I'm the king of beggars.

"Help me move Hank to his new bed," Mal instructs Sara.

"Like this?" Her touch is gentle when she lifts my arm. Her skin is soft, free of callouses.

"On three," Mal counts and they lift me from the chair. My legs are numb and my head spins with the sudden movement. As they hoist me up, my eyes snap open. I let out a roar and tackle Mal to the ground. Sara stumbles and cries out, retreating to a corner in shock. Damn, she really wasn't ready for this.

As I throw a punch at Mal, I open my mouth to scream at him, but my voice is slurred and my movements sluggish. My arm moves slow like it's underwater, and Mal easily sidesteps and shoves me back. I try to get up, but my body is filled with lead weights. I barely make it to my knees before his foot slams into my stomach, knocking the wind from me.

"You ungrateful jerk!" Mal's voice is dripping with betrayal. "I thought we were friends, Hank!"

His eyes are wild like a predator's. He kicks me down again, and before I know it, he's on top of me. My senses are dull and everything's a blur. I feel this hot, searing pain in my right forearm. Looking down, I see Mal biting on it, sinking his teeth into my flesh, blood oozing out. I let out a shriek and try to push him off, but he's like a leech, latched on tight. I swing at him with my free hand, but he dodges and bites down again, this time on my wrist. I can't hold back another scream of agony.

Mal's cool has entirely vanished, and he's cursing and throwing punches. Nothing I do shows any sign of stopping him. Mal's mouth and moustache are smothered with blood—my blood. With my head spinning, I see more of it. More red flowing down my arms and trickling down to the ground. My action has done nothing except give him permission to end me. This is it. If I don't act, I'm finished.

I try to swing for him once more but miss my target, and my fist bounces uselessly off his shoulder. Desperately, I pull my arm back, my elbow connecting with his neck this time.

He groans, but a strange smile envelops his face and his eyes widen like an animal toying with its prey, enjoying the fact its victim is putting up a futile fight. Maybe this is exactly what he was waiting for.

"Nice elbow," he says gleefully, licking his lower lip before pouncing on me once more. This time, both his hands envelop themselves around my neck, cutting off the oxygen to my brain. My arms and legs desperately kick at him, but he's like a rock, unmoving. With every shallow breath, the world around me grows dimmer until I cannot resist anymore. My arms fall to my sides and I draw my last precious breath. Didn't think my life would end like this. I choke and my body begins shuddering.

"Stop, Mal, please, stop!" Sara's voice echoes in the distance, dreamy and miles away.

Mal at last removes his hands. I turn to my side in a coughing fit, desperately trying to ease air into my lungs via my crushed windpipe. It's like sucking a milkshake through a soggy straw.

"Get him back on the chair," he orders Sara. She does as she is told, her movements hesitant and scared. I'm right back where I started, except my predicament has gotten so much worse.

Mal's voice cuts through the fog in my head. There's genuine upset in his voice, like an owner bitten by their faithful hound. He really believed we were friends. "I'm gonna teach you a lesson, Hank."

Then he rummages through the cart and pulls it toward me.

"Daddy, please, he didn't mean it." Sara's voice is desperate. "I think it was the drugs! Made him crazy. It happens all the time."

"Quiet!" Mal snaps at her. "You're in on this too, aren't you? You both wanted to leave me, huh? We'll see about that."

Sara retreats to her corner, her tears unmistakable, even in my dazed state.

I can feel the drugs pulling me under again, the pain and the exhaustion making it hard to stay conscious. I'm fighting it, but I know I'm losing. Perhaps it's better this way. As my eyes close, I can't help but think I might never wake up again, just another one of Mal's victims, chopped up and forgotten. Nobody will be there to mourn me, except Sara. Sara. Sara.

***

"Stay awake, Hank." Mal's voice pulls me back from the extreme edge. It's turned sinister, a stark contrast to his earlier joviality. "You'll want to see this."

He licks his lips, a grotesque smear of my blood across his face, before he picks up something from the cart and strides over to me. In the dim light, I make out the shape of a pair of pliers. My butt clenches in terror.

"What, you gonna try to scare me with those?" I spit out the words with difficulty, defiance in my last stand. I'm as good as dead anyway. "It's gonna be hard to kill me with those."

Mal chuckles, a sound that sends chills down my spine. "Oh, I'm not planning to kill you, Hank," he says. "That'd be too easy. No lessons are learned in death. No, I've got something special in mind., to make sure you never try anything like that again."

"Go to hell," I retort, but Mal just laughs, almost delighted with my continued defiance.

"This will hurt a bit," he says, almost cheerfully, bringing the pliers to my left index finger. Our eyes lock. He latches the nose of his pliers onto my fingernail. I always keep them long because I used to chew them. My way of showing some willpower. He pulls. All I feel at first is pressure, but then he twists back and forth, yanking the nail from its bed. I can't hold back a shrill scream as agony rips through me. I don't want to allow him the satisfaction, but it's impossible.

To him, my pain is a source of pleasure. He keeps his eyes locked on mine, drinking it in.

"I want you to feel every second of this," Mal says, his voice dripping with malice.

I clench my teeth. The nail has not come completely loose. He keeps pulling, slowly, torturously. Every fiber in my body is screaming. I want to beg him to stop, but I won't give him that. I refuse to let him see me crumble and allow him full satisfaction. No, that would show him he has broken me.

Finally, the nail comes free with a tearing noise like Velcro. I fix my gaze on the bloody mess left behind, my skin wrinkled and raw. I gasp for air, the pain overwhelming like a bad burn being rubbed with sandpaper.

Mal examines my torn nail with grim fascination, turning it over in his fingers like it's some sort of trophy.

"Wanna keep that as a souvenir, you sick fuck?" I don't even know how I manage to speak through the overwhelming agony. My body is fighting another battle with my brain, whether I should stay awake or accept the sedative.

Mal looks at the nail, perhaps considering my words. "You know what, Hank? I think I *will* keep it as a souvenir. You've got good, healthy nails. Usually, they come right off with a good pull." He glances at my other fingers. I ball my hands into fists, hiding them from his view, praying he's done.

But Mal's far from finished. "I don't think that one nail's enough for you to learn a proper lesson, Hank."

"I've learned plenty," I shoot back with a sudden desperation to avoid more agony. "I promise I'll never do anything like that again. Sara was right. It's the drugs that made me crazy. You can't blame me for what the drugs made me do, can you?"

Mal just smiles at me, then turns to Sara.

"Sorry, baby," he says to her. "Daddy's still busy. There's food in the blue bag. Help yourself." Sara just stays frozen, not moving an inch toward the bag. Who could think of eating right now? Who but a maniac like Mal.

"Are you ready for some more, Hank?" Mal leans in towards my hand. *What is he going to do now?* The next thing I know, Mal's tongue is slithering over the blood on my hand. I gag, then let out a scream—the loudest sound I've ever made. I want to puke.

"Oh, Hank, you really haven't learned about not resisting me, have you?" Mal taunts as he straightens himself, clamping the pliers onto my middle finger.

I brace myself for the agony.

7

Waking up on the thin mattress the next day feels like luxury compared to the hard chair. I can move my legs, which is something, but the right one's chained to the wall. My eyes follow the chain. It appears to go through the thick iron hoop that Mal attached to the wall earlier and then continues to Sara's leg. We're both attached to the same chain, and if either of us wants to walk somewhere, the other would need to shorten their side by walking towards the iron hoop.

"You were out for ages." Sara's voice is soft, concerned.

Thankfully, I passed out the moment he started pulling off the second nail. The pain in my fingers has dialed down to a throbbing eight out of ten, but I don't let it show. I don't want Sara to see the pain I'm in, not on top of all she's dealing with. "I didn't expect to wake up full stop, if you want the truth."

I examine my hand. The bite marks are a brutal reminder of Mal's hospitality. I fight the nausea I feel when I see the bloody globs which were once my fingernails. Three are gone. I guess two wasn't enough, either. Perhaps I fought on, even without being conscious. I gulp down and steady my face.

"I tried to stop him," Sara says, her voice cracking. "He just kept going, even after you passed out. But he's never been this kind to the others."

"Kind?" I scoff. "I think we've got different opinions when it comes to kindness."

"He's never let the others last more than a few hours," Sara says. "There's some reason he's keeping you alive. Maybe it's for the same reason he spared me."

"What reason is that?" I ask. "Because you play along with his sick game?"

"Well, yeah," Sara says. She sounds offended and I regret my choice of words, but the pain is filling me with bitterness. "I just wanted to stay alive, Hank. And anyway, what the hell happened to our plan?"

"My bad," I admitted. "I got ahead of myself," I say, trying to ignore the pain thrumming through my fingertips and up my arm.

Sara looks at me for a few long seconds. "It's okay."

The light above us flickers ominously, then turns back to normal. Sara doesn't react, so I think nothing of it.

"You must be starving," Sara says after another few seconds and offers me a plastic grocery bag. I think Mal brought it inside earlier. I don't really remember. The smell of food hits me and my stomach growls in response.

"Thanks," I say, mustering a weak smile. I rummage through the bag, finding an assortment of store-bought sandwiches: ham and cheese, BLT, tuna and mayo. My eyes skim past them to some fruit and water bottles. I grab a bottle, open it, and gulp it down in three greedy gulps, the water soothing my parched throat. Feeling a bit more alive with the hydration, I tear into the ham and cheese sandwich, devouring it in just a few bites. I had no idea how damn hungry I was.

"Easy there," Sara warns me, pulling the bag away. "We've got to make the food last." She ties the bag up and sets it aside, then moves closer to me. "Let me see those wounds." She already has Mal's pouch of medical supplies open beside her. "You won't last long enough to escape if you don't take care of yourself."

I can't tell if she really believes what she's saying, but it lifts my spirits a little.

"Thank you," I murmur while I examine my injuries. The wound on my right forearm looks worse than I thought, swollen, and crusted with dried blood.

She begins to clean the wound at the back of my head, but I can tell she's struggling to keep her composure at the sight of all the blood.

"Here, let me do it," I say, taking over. The cloth comes away stained red, which I toss into a bag. I probe the stitches at the back of my head, revulsion crawling up my spine. Thank God I can't see myself.

After I'm done cleaning the wound, Sara clears her throat. "Hank," she says, standing with a towel in her hands. I don't even know where she grabbed it from when the room is so derelict and empty. "I need a shower."

"Sure," I say, unsure what else to add. "Um, what do you want me to... I'll just..." Instead of finishing my sentence, I turn to face the wall, giving her some privacy.

"Thanks," Sara says. "Won't be long."

"Take your time," I tell her. "Promise I won't look."

"Do you read?" Sara asks suddenly. Such a normal question takes me by surprise.

"Not really," I admit. "More of a music and movies guy."

"Well, maybe give this a try, anyway." She hands me a hardback book titled *Keeper of the Genesis*, with a picture of the Sphinx on the cover. "It's a good read."

"You think so?" I ask, weighing whether to invest time in such triviality when I need to regroup and come up with a better plan. But then again, there's a lot of time to think down here, and not much to occupy my mind except thoughts of revenge.

"Well, I liked it," Sara says. "It's not like we've got much else to do here. Might take your mind off our... our predicament." I know she's only trying to lighten the mood, but she's somehow voiced my exact thoughts,

I accept the book with a nod, then turn away again to face the wall. A few seconds pass. The soft rattle of water hitting the stone slabs fills the room. It's a nice change from the silence. Like an instrumental song or those CDs with whale sounds or tropical rainstorms to help you sleep. Sara starts humming to herself. She can hold a tune pretty well. I open the book. I can't remember the last time that I read something for leisure besides newspapers and magazines, maybe not since school. My eyes struggle to adjust to the lines of letters. My eyes want to do anything but read. I stare at the front page but don't pay any attention to the text.

I must have zoned out, because when Sara comes back into view, she's finished wrapping the towel around herself, and her hair is wet, with droplets of water clinging to her pale skin.

Flustered, I look away immediately and start reading.

"How's the book?" she asks me in a somewhat cheerful tone, wrinkling her nose in a cute, childish way.

"Oh, it's good," I lie. I haven't even made it past the first sentence, which I've read three times now.

"You should take a shower, too," Sara says to me. "You'll feel much better."

Our hands brush as she hands me a fresh towel and I feel the warmth of her soft hands for a second, catching the coconut scent of shampoo in her hair. I feel a little shy about showing my body. The physique I had in my twenties and thirties is long gone, replaced with a bit of a potbelly. I glance behind me several times to make sure she's not looking and then undress. The warm water feels like heaven until it hits my wounds, and I wince, letting out a slight whimper. When I turn once more, Sara is laying down, facing the wall away from me, buried deep in whatever book she's reading.

I take a grubby bar of soap off the floor and rub it generously all over my body, careful when going around my fresh wounds. I try not to get my head wet because of Mal's recent attempts at stitching me up. When I'm done with the soap, I wash the blood off under the tap. The water at my feet is all red too. It looks like a scene from Carrie. Honestly, it's horrifying. I'm not one to feel sick easily, but the sight of it, the metallic smell, and the burn from my inflamed flesh almost makes me vomit.

I spend no more time washing than necessary to rinse off the soap. I turn the tap off, carefully pat myself dry, and put some fresh clothes on. Mal bought me a pair of stiff, stonewashed jeans, which thankfully fit fine around the waist. His estimation was pretty much spot on, although they are a little long, so I fold up the bottom twice over. In the plastic bag, I also have three T-shirts to choose from. I go for the plain black one, figuring it will hide the blood better if I start bleeding again. My old clothes are barely recognizable now that they are all hard-stained with blood. I might as well chuck them in the bin. As I rise to carry them over, my chain pulls me back, and I hear a disgruntled tut from Sara.

"Dude, if you want to go somewhere, tell me first," she complains. "I don't want to be yanked around like a rag doll. Not by you, too."

"Sorry," I say, mentally hitting myself in the head.

"It's fine," Sara says as she stands up and takes a few steps closer to the middle of our chain divider. She sits back down with her book still in her hands.

Once I've chucked away the old clothes, I'm overcome by sudden weakness. The past twenty-four hours have been damn hard, and my body's screaming out to relax. I look around the basement to see if there's anything else I've missed. Anything at all. But it really is just a damp old basement. Aside from the pile of books that Mal had gotten Sara, and the bags of clothes and the food in the corner, there's nothing else here.

I sit back down on my mattress and pick up my book on the Sphinx. Might as well give it another go. There's nothing else to do.

8

Mal is back in the basement with us, sporting his signature loose tie look. I think it's been two or three days. I really don't know. Time no longer has any meaning without daylight to mark its passing. Some of my back teeth have begun to ache. The pain tends to come and go every few weeks, and now it's back with a vengeance. I've been praying that it's nothing, but I figured the doc was going to tell me to get them pulled. I was worried about finding the money to book a check-up, let alone the work the dentist would recommend. Oh, to have such trivial concerns again. I'll never take anything for granted—if I ever make it out of this crummy basement alive.

Being cooped up in this small space for what seemed like days has placed me in a state of claustrophobia and I've spent recent hours mostly staring into space, without a coherent thought in my head. Occasionally, my mind has tried to formulate another impossible escape plan, but it seems futile. I've also thought about Sara. If the few days I've spent here feels like this, I can't even imagine what a month must have been like for her. I'm in true admiration of her now. I don't see her as a young girl, but a strong woman for what she has endured. She and I engage in conversation and, of course, being chained together has made us closer. If I ever get free, then meeting Sara will be the only bright side I've had from this experience.

Thinking about her makes me fantasize about what I would do to Mal if I got another chance at freedom. I'd inflict every bit of pain he has inflicted upon me and Sara. I'd make him suffer like he has made us suffer. For her sake, not mine. I don't care about Hank Griffin anymore. I've no idea how I'm gonna do it, but I'll make Mal pay for what he did. I don't even know whether it's night or day in this cramped-up basement, or even how long I've been trapped here. I only know that it's getting colder and colder by day, so the weather in the world above must be getting colder, too.

Strangely, Mal's in a jolly mood when he comes bounding down the ladder. At least for the time being, I decide that I'm going to avoid doing anything to hinder that. I'm not eager to receive fresh bites from my host or another round of *pull the nail*. The current bite wounds are more swollen than yesterday, both on my hand and arm. I still feel his jaw biting down against my skin—piercing it—drawing blood.

My head's still pulsating from the hit to the back of my head. Looking into the tiny makeup mirror Sara gave me,

I can see that my entire face is pretty busted up now—got bruises all over. Mal gave me some pills to take the edge off, but the pain remains. Thanks to Sara, the vicious bites on my arm and hand are now bandaged up, but all it really does is mask what Mal's done.

Mal notices me eyeing the bloodied bandages. "Hope the bites are healing okay, Hank," he says. The way he puts it, one might even think it was some rabid animal who bit me, not him. I give him a nod and say nothing. What is there to say?

"So, I've been thinking," Mal says, rubbing his hands together. "Christmas is coming, and I was asking myself, what would Sara and Hank want for Christmas?"

Freedom from this stinking basement?

Sara sits up with her back straight, listening attentively. I know she's just playing along, but I don't want to be part of Mal's twisted reality. Sara's eyes fall on mine. She blinks once, as if asking me to follow her. I shake my head. Despite my earlier vow, I can't play the part of a slave. Fuck that.

"So, you'll be pleased to know that I've decided to let both of you live with me!" Mal announces happily, looking at us like we are his loyal audience. "Hank, you must have been terrified and I'm sorry for putting you through all of this. I figured you didn't really want to hurt me. You were just scared that I was going to kill you or messed up from the anesthetic." I say nothing and let him ramble on, wearing a half-smile he must take for obedience, but is really from fantasizing about ripping his throat out. "I know that this place isn't exactly a dream, so with your permission, I'd like to help you decorate it and make it feel more homely."

How am I supposed to react to his sick mind games? I suppose after my fiasco the other day, acting dumb is my only shot at gaining his trust. Or making him believe his efforts to work me over have broken me. I try to think positively—he's keeping us alive, for now. But for how long, I don't know. After all, he is a psychopath. You never know what he might do. Even if he says he has decided to let us live with him, what does he really mean by that? He could flip and kill us any day, any hour, any minute.

Mal is expecting an answer from us, but the only thing on my mind right now is the thought of grabbing a fistful of his hair and bashing his head up against the cold stone walls. I open my mouth, hoping that some words might come out of it, but nothing does. I'm hoping that Sara will speak for the both of us.

Sara stands up. "Mal, this is the best present ever, thank you!" she says with fake excitement. I look at her alarmingly. Sometimes, I can't tell whether she's pretending or not. I guess she's that good of an actor. If she makes it to LA, I think she should do some auditions. She's got the talent. Sara then opens her arms wide and walks over to Mal to give him a hug. I quickly shuffle towards the wall so that her side of chain is long enough to reach him.

"You deserve it, baby," Mal says softly into her ear whilst caressing her hair.

"Yeah, thanks Mal," I add, the words sticking in my throat and making me want to throw up. Seeing Mal's arms wrapped around Sara makes me squeeze my fists into balls. I imagine Olivia in her place. My innocent little girl, at the mercy of a killer, and me, unable to protect her. I have to keep thinking of a way out. I have to. I may be a nobody, with my best days behind me, but Sara has just begun to live, to chase her dreams of becoming an actress. She's been through far too much pain for her age—she deserves somebody to fight for her.

"Trust me, you're both going to love it here!" Mal says enthusiastically. "Just give it time." The last words were meant for me, and he stares directly at me as he delivers them. He reaches into his fleece pocket and takes out a pen and paper. "I thought we'd brainstorm together, come up with some ideas. And then I'll go to the store today to get the bits."

I remind myself that in missing person scenarios like this, the police take their sweet time to find missing people. Given that they're already patrolling the area, everything is staring them in the face. Surely, it's only a matter of when not if they connect the dots. I may not even have to fight my way out. Maybe I just have to keep Mal at bay and delay him from hurting us until help arrives. Or worse than hurting.

"Hey, Mal," I speak up, trying not to arouse suspicion by staying silent. "It's getting pretty cold in here. Don't you think some heaters would be nice?"

I see his smile stretch even more. "Of course!" he remarks. "It is getting rather chilly, isn't it? First morning frost of the year today."

Sara nods as he writes the first suggestion down. Neither I nor Sara voice another opinion. Instead, we watch Mal's pen scratch the paper absentmindedly, and murmur our submissive acknowledgement any time he speaks.

"Come on guys, don't be shy now," Mal urges. "It's Christmas season and this is your new home! I want you both to feel comfortable here. Don't worry about the prices, just tell me what you guys want. I have the money." He chuckles.

Where exactly is this money coming from? Then again, he does own a motel, so he must have inherited money. Unless the bastard won the lottery.

"If it's not too much to ask," I speak up again, keeping my tone polite. "It would be nice to have some music in here. Maybe a radio?" With me and Sara missing, my bet is that every station in the state is talking about the case.

"Missing your country music already, are ya?" Mal jokes.

"You know me, Mal. I'm a sucker for that sad, lonely trucker music and it sure would help keep my spirits up." I'm one step away from batting my eyelids like some Disney character.

"Sure thing bud, consider it done."

"Thanks."

"A television would be nice," Sara chips in, with a quiver in her voice.

Mal thinks about this for a moment. "I could get an old television with a DVD player if you'd like." He leans forward, full of interest now. "Both of you, quickly give me five movies you like."

"*The Princess Diaries!*" Sara blurts out. "Oh, and *Notting Hill*."

"*The Good, the Bad and the Ugly*," I contribute, intentionally looking at him as I say the last word.

"How about *La La Land*?"

"*Gran Torino*," I counter. "Clint Eastwood's masterpiece."

"That's five!" Mal announces before we get carried away. "Next?"

"Maybe some art supplies?" Sara suggests.

"You got it, darling," Mal says, giving her a wink.

That sentence alone brings reality crushing back. I remind myself not to let my guard down. Can't figure the guy out at all. He kidnaps us, and now he's offering to buy us Christmas gifts? He doesn't even seem bothered that I tried to fight him a few days ago.

"You should buy something for yourself too, Daddy," Sara suggests. "Or something that we could all do together. A game, perhaps."

I give her a look to say *what the hell are you doing?* She shoots me a forced smile, making me remember that she's following through the first step of the plan as we agreed—gain Mal's trust. Maybe, just maybe, we'll get another shot at freedom. I must be patient.

"How about a puzzle?" Mal suggests awkwardly, as though he's embarrassed. *Well, that's a first,* I think. "And maybe some board games?"

"Hell yeah, that would be awesome!" Sara's enthusiasm almost makes me forget it's all an act. But I can tell that she's dying inside at the idea.

Mal turns to me to see my reaction. I nod at him. "Sounds good, Mal," I say. "How about Cluedo?" If he realizes the suggestion is a bit of a jab, then he doesn't show it. Instead, he smiles, and I see him writing something down on his paper.

"A murder mystery game, good choice," Mal chuckles. My dark humor must have gone over his head. "Let's also add chess, and one more, perhaps?" He looks at Sara expectedly.

"Scrabble," she suggests.

"Scrabble," Mal says, writing before he looks over to me again. "How are the clothes, by the way, Hank?"

"They're good," I say with a shrug. Mal folds the paper, about it put it back in his pocket. "There is just one other thing, Mal. We could really use with something to cook with. I don't think store-bought sandwiches will keep us healthy."

Mal gives me a funny look and shakes his finger. "No silly business, Hank," he says. "I don't want the house going into blazes if you have a hiccup with a gas canister. So no can do. Sara knows that everything I cook, I do on a grill outside in the courtyard."

"Not a gas stove. I wouldn't expect you to buy that," I say, trying to bring back any shred of trust this maniac might still have for me. "Perhaps something like an induction cooktop? They are a bit pricier, maybe fifty bucks or so but at least you'll have your peace of mind. And I could keep me and Sara fed well if you could bring us the ingredients."

"Buying raw ingredients would be way cheaper than getting those expensive pre-made sandwiches," Sara adds in.

This appears to win Mal over and he ponders the suggestion. When his attention drifts, Sara eyes me carefully. I give her a reassuring nod.

Finally, Mal looks at us and nods. He unfolds the piece of paper out and notes it down. "Okay, guys," he says with a chuckle. "It's going to be an expensive Christmas for Uncle Mal, but I think you two are worth it. Just don't make me regret it, okay?"

"Thank you, Daddy," says Sara.

"Thanks Mal," I force myself to add.

Mal checks his watch but doesn't say the time out loud. "I should pop over to the store now before it closes," he says. "We can have dinner together today. I've got some nice, fresh meat frozen out back. I'll cook it up on our new induction stove when I return." He gives me a wink. "Hope you guys like pork."

I smile. Then, my eyes dart towards the door he pointed to. It must be a walk-in freezer, like they have in restaurants to preserve food. I bet he has all sorts of medicine and food in there. Maybe even something I could use against him. If that's where he takes his victims to kill them, then there must be weapons. Sara told me he doesn't always come back, so there has to be another exit.

I'm deep in thought, to the point that I don't even notice him walk away or climb the ladder. I blink and snap back to reality at the sound of the hatch closing above as Mal leaves Sara and I alone again, if only for a little while.

We look at each other. Sara notices the look on my face and is expecting the question.

"We need to see what's behind that door. I bet there's a tunnel, or another exit that he takes to wherever he disposes of the bodies," I say. "And I bet there could be other rooms through there."

"I guess so. No one he's taken in there has ever come out, so he must have some way of getting them out of the motel without anyone noticing. All I know is that he keeps a lot of food in there. Mostly meat, fish, frozen stuff."

"Okay, so the best thing for us to do would be to convince Mal to show us the room. Then we'll know exactly what's back there. That could be the key to our escape."

"I agree," she says. "He goes in there all the time."

"Do you ever hear anything?"

She shakes her head. "No, it's soundproof. I can never hear a sound once he closes the door."

Not even the screams. She doesn't say it, but the sentiment hangs in the air between us.

"And I reckon if there is nothing that can help us in that room, we could lock him inside. All we'd need is to find a way to get the keys off him without him noticing. Once he's trapped, we'll be able to climb up the hatch."

Sara keeps nodding, as though seriously contemplating our half-baked escape plan.

When she doesn't speak, I ask, "What's on your mind?"

"I'm scared. Part of me doesn't want to know what's behind that door."

"I'm sure it's nothing. Don't worry, we'll get out of here. I promise. Hang in there."

Sara gives me a smile and lays down on her mattress, looking into nothingness. She's right, as usual. I've thought the same thing. It's like the grand prize in the world's worst gameshow. Mal is the malignant host, and he wants to show us what's behind door number one.

I close my eyes for a bit to fill my mind with something positive, but quickly drift into a daydream. Sally strides into view. We're walking down a street that my mind's constructed, hand-in-hand. It's a warm day, with people walking up and down the footpath lined with shops.

"I miss you, Sally."

Her beautiful lashes flutter. "Aw, darling, I miss you too."

"I want to join you, up there," I gesture up towards the cloudless sky.

She brings her soft hands up to my cheeks and smiles. "It's not your time, my love, not yet."

"When will it be time?"

"Don't think so much about death, Hank. It's life you should be thinking of. In the meantime, I will grow more beautiful plants in our garden. I can't wait for you to see it."

I don't speak another word, for I'm lost in Sally's eyes. Lost, like the first time we met.

***

I pick up my book and turn to the first page, determined to get through at least a few pages to distract myself. The first paragraph is hard to follow. My eyes just skim over the words and by the time I get to the end, I haven't absorbed a thing. I start over, reading the first, then the second paragraph, using my finger to follow the words, real slow like a kid learning to read. I move to the third and fourth paragraph, and before I know it, I'm on to the second chapter.

The book's about the Great Sphinx and the pyramids, but not the obvious stuff they taught us in school. Hancock, the guy who wrote it, has some wild ideas. He's talking about these ancient places being way older than we think, built by some forgotten civilization. It's a bit out there but I gotta admit, it's gripping. Perhaps he means an alien civilization. Wild!

I never put much stock in history. I always figured the past is the past, and all that matters is what's coming. But this Hancock fella, he's making me think. He ties many things together—star patterns, old myths and relics dug up from the earth. Makes you wonder if what we know is just a drop in the ocean. The old adage goes smart people are the ones that know they don't know nothing, while the real dummies are the ones that think they know it all.

Reading this book in this godforsaken basement, it's like traveling without moving. My body's here, but my mind's wandering through these ancient ruins, trying to piece together a puzzle that's thousands of years old. I can almost see myself there, walking beside these massive stone structures, feeling small in the grand scheme of things.

It's funny, in a way. Here I am, caught up in Mal's twisted world and yet this book's got me pondering about time and civilizations long gone. Makes my problems seem small, almost petty. Plus, it's a good escape. It's like

Hancock saying, 'Look, there's more to the world than you realize.' And right now, I need that—something to remind me there's a world beyond these walls, vast and full of mysteries. It takes me back to the wonder of childhood, reading my comics, and my war stories, and science fiction magazines, my mind open and alive to possibility. I didn't know it then, but being a child is true happiness.

Sara's breathing softly nearby and I'm here, lost in ancient Egypt, thanks to a book. Ain't life strange? I close my eyes and feel myself transported. My bare feet feel the warm sand beneath them. I take a deep breath in. The wind softly blows against my face. When my eyes re-open, I'm met with the most amazing sight. The three great pyramids. The Sphinx. The surrounding temples. They're all even higher than they look in the pictures. It absolutely boggles my mind that this was all built by human hands.

I imagine the pyramids as they were thousands of years ago. Smooth, covered in polished white limestone. A camel struts by me, and now I am surrounded by the people of ancient times. I stand at the center of a lively bazaar. To my left is a market stand full of large baskets of fresh fruit. To my right, there is a stall that sells papyrus and ink. I look down at myself. I am dressed head to toe in fine white linen.

A sudden gust of wind blows a grain of sand in my eyes. I rub them, and re-appear in the dark, solemn basement, with the book in front of me. I turn the page to the next chapter.

9

Mal returns a few hours later. He passes box after box to me down the open hatch. I put the boxes down carefully, one after another. What choice is there but to play along as usual? Looking at the boxes, I try to sum up how much all of this crap must have cost. Looks no less than three hundred dollars.

Sara's mood seems lifted by the delivery. I mean, it doesn't hurt to have some distractions down here at last. But these little delicacies are like keeping sheep happy before their slaughter, so I keep reminding myself not to buy it.

Once the last of the boxes are all inside the basement, Mal lowers the ladder through the hatch and climbs down to join us. Smiling with glee, he tidies up his already neatly combed hair and pulls a box cutter from his pocket. My mind adds yet another possible way for us to gain our freedom when Mal's guard drops. However, I also notice the way he smartly positions himself on the other side of the room, just far enough to avoid me from reaching him if

I were to charge towards him and try to grab him. Behind Mal's *kind* and *generous* alter ego is a smart, calculated psychopath whom I should never underestimate.

"Let's get these opened up, shall we?" Mal says enthusiastically, rubbing his mustache.

I watch him cut the top of the boxes open with the box cutter and then slide them towards me so I can take the contents out. It's almost like he doesn't want to spoil the surprise of what's in them, even though we already know. In the first box is the television. It's an old thing, one of those bulky, gray early generation combo television and DVD players. I carefully take it out and place it on the floor by my side, along with the cables and remotes that come with it.

"Do us a favor, Hank," Mal calls out to me. "Flat pack the cardboard boxes for me, will you?"

I give him a nod and do as he's asked, keeping a close eye on every step he makes. If he treads just a few steps closer, I may just have to take up the opportunity to take the box cutter from him. Unlike last time, I haven't been dosed with his medication. The more sensible part of my brain tells me to stick to what Sara and I agreed—to gain Mal's trust first. My mind flickers again to the next thought, hearing a set of keys jingle against the side of his jeans on a carabiner. I shake my head clear. *Stop overthinking, Hank.*

It looks like he brought these plain boxes with him to the stores, then placed everything he purchased inside them. I suppose it is a smart move in case someone staying in the motel gets a little curious and decides to peak through their windows.

The next box has the DVDs on the top. They're pre-owned and have labels on each of them with the name of the shop he bought them from. I recognize the name. I'm pretty sure I drove past it on the way to the motel. It's probably forty minutes from here. Below the DVDs are the board games and puzzles. It's clear that he wants to spend more time with us. Or maybe with just Sara. I really don't know why he is keeping me alive or why he cares about what I want. I'm still trying to figure him out, but it's clear that he's lonely and desperately in need of human affection. And while he thinks of Sara as a daughter in some twisted way, maybe he thinks of me as a friend. Perhaps this is why I'm still breathing.

The next box we open has the portable heater. It's one of those cheap plastic ones with a fan inside, but as long as it keeps me warm, I ain't complaining. The art supplies are in the last box, as well as the induction hob and some pans. Thank God. We may get some decent food at last.

"You're welcome," Mal says, seeing me eye the hob.

I mutter my thanks while neatly laying everything out on the floor. Despite how much I despise the situation I'm in, I have more possessions here than I have back in Texas. I sold pretty much everything I own, and the proceeds only ate a fraction of the medical bills. They're still stacked in a pile the height of a tower, chipping away at my bank account each month. How long before the overdue notices pile up in the letterbox, now I'm not there to pay them?

I see one more box behind Mal. This one's bulky and wide.

"What's in there?" I ask, my curiosity finally getting the better of me.

"Oh, you'll like this one," says Mal, putting his box cutter into his back pocket. "We can put it up together before I start cooking. Might need some help, Hank."

As we unpack it, I see an instruction manual for a small dining table. It's one of those Asian style ones that are low down near to the ground, so there's no need for chairs. I glance over at Mal several times, weighing out the risk of wrestling him to the ground. He's far enough from me that he'd have time to push himself away before I reached him. Best not to risk it. If Sara knocked him over the head with one of the table legs right now, that would subdue him long enough for me to pull him to me, but I don't have any way of communicating my plan to her, so I simmer down the idea, for now.

"Thought it'd be barbaric for you two to eat food on the floor," says Mal.

"Thank you," Sara says as she skips over, handing one of the table legs to him. We attach the legs on and flip the table over.

It's solid oak, pretty sturdy. Mal gestures for me to pass him the induction hob. I hand it to him instead of smashing him over the head with it. The thing isn't solid enough to do the kind of damage I need. He places it on the table, inserts the batteries and walks off to the door at the end of the room. I hear the rattle of keys. Must be at least five different ones. He finds the right one, inserts it into the keyhole, and opens the door, just wide enough for him to fit through. I watch as he walks inside and closes it behind him.

Neither me nor Sara say a word while he's away in case he overhears. Instead, we wait patiently, looking through the myriad of things he's purchased for us. I look over the descriptions on the back of the DVDs. Thank God for the two Clint Eastwood flicks. I absolutely love them, especially *Gran Torino*. It even made me cry the first time I watched it. Hadn't cried over a goddamn movie since *E.T.*

About five minutes later, my eyes flick up as the door swings open. Mal's holding a plate with what looks like three generously sized steaks, frozen.

"I've been looking forward to share this with someone," Mal says proudly, showing us the food like it's some game he hunted. "Got these at a great price from a butcher. Been waiting for a special occasion. The guy that runs it is a legend. Known the guy for fifteen years—Bill sure knows his meat!"

I want nothing more than to tell him to shut the fuck up. But my stomach rumbles in disagreement. I haven't eaten a proper meal in almost a week. If we're to escape from this hellhole, we'll need strength, which means food.

Sara takes me by the hand and sits me down alongside her at the new table. Our chains are extended to the max—I wouldn't be able to even reach out my hand to the other side of the table if I tried. Mal's smart, I'll give him that.

Sitting quietly, we watch Mal as he turns the induction hob on, places a frying pan and slaps a small slab of butter on. It sizzles as the butter fully melts and spreads. The sound and smell of the butter makes me think of the times when Sally used to make pancakes for breakfast. I can't believe I ever took such things for granted.

Mal takes the first steak and gently places it on the pan. It begins to crackle after a few seconds, the smell of frying meat filling the basement, making me salivate. It's so good it even masks the smell of dampness in this place. Mal and I make eye contact over the table.

"This first one's for you, the newest addition to the family," Mal says to me, flipping the steak over onto the other side. He hands me a knife and fork. To my surprise, they're metal, although the knife is not serrated. "Be careful with these," he says, but there's no malice in his voice. Realistically, there's not much I nor Sara could do with blunt cutlery. Nevertheless, I'm surprised that he's so confident that we won't make a bid to escape. I mustn't take him for a fool. Every move he makes is calculated. The chances are, he's testing us. He's always testing us.

Sara sits silently beside me, her eyes darting between the steak and Mal. There's a tension in the air as if we're all playing parts in some deranged play.

"Keep an eye on the steak," Mal says. "I'm going to grab some salt and pepper. Can't be eating unseasoned meat." He stands up from where he is sitting.

Once he's on the other side of the room with his back turned, Sara whispers to me, "Don't do anything stupid."

Mal is back seconds later, scratching his mustache as he takes the sizzling steak out of the frying pan, placing it neatly on a plate. Then, with a smile on his face like a father preparing food for his children, he sprinkles a generous quantity of salt and pepper on it. After a satisfactory look at his handiwork, he slides the plate across the table to me.

"Enjoy," he says, seemingly eager to see me take a bite.

I look down at the steak, cooked to perfection, golden brown on the outside, probably juicy on the inside. It's a mouthwatering sight, but the thought of having a bite makes me feel like I'm conforming to his rules. Here I am, chained up to a wall with another man cooking me food.

I cut a small piece off with my knife and pierce it with my fork. With two pairs of eyes watching me, time seems to run slower than ever. I have a moment of hesitation before placing it in my mouth. The flavor hits me, rich and savory, almost good enough to make me forget that I'm not at a diner. I chew slowly, savoring what might be my last meal. Mal watches me intently, waiting for my reaction.

"It's good," I manage to say, although it feels a betrayal.

Mal's eyes beam with excitement. "Told you," he says. "Nothing beats fresh produce."

Not long after, Sara gets a steak of her own and starts cutting it up as quickly as possible before biting down. We sit there, eating in silence, a bizarre semblance of a family meal.

As I continue with the next piece, a thought slithers its way into my mind. Sharpening the knife into a blade using the side of a wall might work if I have the luxury of time.

Mal breaks the silence with some small talk. "Did you ever get lonely out there, driving all day and night by yourself, Hank?"

I shrug, trying to appear nonchalant. "Sometimes," I say. "But I like the peace and quiet." I gulp down another piece of meat. "I like it when it's just me and my truck."

"Why'd you name her Midnight?" Sara chimes in, her voice a little stronger than before.

"Because of her dark paint job. Also, I do most of my driving at night," I say. I try to give everyone a friendly smile, but it feels forced.

Mal leans back, stroking his moustache thoughtfully, before locking eyes with Sara. "Hank here doesn't have anyone waiting for him back home, so Midnight was the only thing he could rely on," he announces, as though he's doing a podcast. "But now he has us! I'm sure he's much happier now. Aren't you, Hank?"

Mal's condescending words make me grip my fork harder. I feel Sara's leg touch mine, and when my eyes briefly meet hers, I loosen my grip. If I was to stab him in the neck right now, he'd back away towards the far wall and we'd still be stuck here, still chained to the wall, with no way of getting out. Within a week or two, we'd be goners.

Mal's gaze lingers on me, probing, but then turns to Sara. "And what about you, darling?" he asks her. "Tell Hank about your dreams, your plans before... Well, before you found your new home and your *real* family." He smiles at her sweetly. I can almost feel the meat coming back up my throat.

Sara hesitates, then speaks softly. "Well, as you know, I was going to move to LA to get a fresh start. The plan was to take a year figuring out what to do whilst working as a barista or something."

I try to offer her a supportive smile. "That sounds sensible."

She nods. "I don't have any grand plan for life, but I think that moving to a new place, meeting new people can open up your eyes to new things," she says. "I'd love to give theatre acting a go."

"Dreams, ambitions... It's all so fleeting," Mal says with a chuckle. "The world out there is so vacuous. But here, with me, you both have a purpose. Isn't that better than chasing shadows?"

I clench my jaw, feeling anger bubble up. "Some might say being free to chase those shadows is what life's all about."

Mal tilts his head, considering my words. "Freedom's overrated, Hank," he says carefully. "Here, there are no uncertainties, no disappointments. I'll provide everything you need."

The audacity of his words makes my skin crawl. I want to lash out and tell him he's a psychopath who deserves to die in agony, lying in a pool of his own blood, but I hold back. Anger won't help us here now. Not in this situation.

Sara looks down at her hands. It's clear she's heard this spiel before.

The conversation drifts, Mal talking about his vision for our little *family*. It's delusional and utterly detached from reality. But as he speaks, it dawns on me this is more than simple captivity for him; it's his twisted version of a perfect world. I wonder if he used to capture animals and trap them with him as a kid? These psychos often start with animals, if any of the true-life murder programs I've watched are to be believed.

As Mal continues to ramble, I study him, thinking about how I could get my hands on his set of keys without him knowing. One of those keys would surely unlock the shackle on my leg. Another would let us unlock the metal door to see what was on the other side.

"You know, I've always craved a family," he says. "My own was... let's say, less than ideal."

Sara, her voice barely audible, plays along. "What was your family like, Daddy?"

Mal's eyes glaze over, as though lost in memories. "Dysfunctional, Sara. My father was a cruel man and my mother, well, she was too weak to stand up to him. I learned early on that if you want something in life, you have to take control."

I listen, keeping my expression neutral while I mentally note every detail. Poor Mal was starved of love. Weren't we all? I've met people who come from messed up families and they weren't psychopaths like Mal.

"And you, Hank?" Mal suddenly turns to me. "You must understand the loneliness of the road. You know, the need for something more."

I nod, weighing my words. "The road can be lonely, sure," I admit. "But it's nothing like what you've got going on here." I don't want Mal to get too comfortable. I want him to know that I won't truly back down. I'll play along, but I won't be suppressed totally. Bend but don't break.

Mal chuckles, his sharp gaze resting on mine. "Ah, but you see, Hank, here, I'm in control," he says. "No unpredictability, no chaos. Just us, living as we should."

Sara shifts uncomfortably. "And... and we're your family now?"

Switching his gaze from mine, Mal beams at Sara. "Exactly!" he says to her. "Here, you're safe and loved. I'll never let anything bad happen to you! Deep down, you know yourself that there is no future for you in Los Angeles. No one who wants to become a movie star actually makes it. Not unless you have connections. And if your fallback plan is to be a barista, that's hardly a proper life."

I fight the urge to scoff at his obscene comments.

"I decided long ago I'd create my own destiny, make my own family," Mal continues. "A family that can't hurt me, that can't leave me. I didn't expect it to start like this with the two of you, but life is full of unexpected events, isn't it?"

It's clear Mal's past has twisted him, driven him into this madness. His idea of family is a prison of his own making. I can't help but feel a surge of anger at his delusion, although I try to fight it, knowing what will happen if my anger explodes. I attempt to water down my feelings, and I think carefully before choosing my words to ask my next question.

"And what if we don't want to be part of this *family* of yours, Mal?" I can't help myself.

Mal's expression darkens, and he leans in closer. "But why wouldn't you?" he asks me in a tone brimming with danger. "Here, you have everything you need. Food, shelter, company. The outside world is harsh and unforgiving. In

117

here, you're safe. When's the last time you had a steak this good? I promise you'll be fed like a king every day!"

The conversation continues, Mal detailing his plans for our life together. It's a twisted vision, a blend of domestic normalcy and deranged fantasy. As he speaks, I begin to understand this is more than just a game for him—it's his reality.

Eventually, Mal clears the table. He places all the plates and cutlery down on the floor by the shower. "Clean this up when you get a chance. I'll be back in a minute with dessert," he says cheerfully before he climbs up the ladder and disappears through the hatch.

"He's completely lost his mind," Sara whispers once the hatch slams shut.

"He can't be serious about all that family nonsense, can he?"

"I guess the bright side to all this is that he doesn't plan to kill us. I mean, he wouldn't kill his family, right?"

I look at her but don't respond. Before I can dwell on my thoughts, I hear the hatch open once again and see Mal climbing back down with a cheesecake in hand.

"*Bon appétit!*"

10

A nightmare shakes me awake. I kick away my duvet and sit up, covered in sweat. Nothing unusual, really. Not a week goes by in my life without at least one or two demons entering my dreams. They're pretty much a part of my life. I've thought about these nightmares a lot, actually. Had plenty of time to contemplate things, being a trucker. My theory is that the demons are trying to pull me down towards hell. A reminder of the countless times I've thought about taking my own life.

Suicide is a coward's way out, but the only thing holding me back is knowing that ending things kills any chance for me to see my Sally again. Heaven does not open its gates to those who take their own life. I'm not super religious, but that's what I believe. It's a real pickle. I have been on the verge of suicide several times in the past, but Sally's voice has always stopped me in the nick of time. But this is a world I no longer want to be a part of.

Since becoming Mal's prisoner in this damp basement, Sally's voice has grown fainter each day. There's no way for me to end my life here, even if I wanted to. If I could figure out how, my thoughts are constantly revolving around Sara and her safety. She drives me to keep fighting, gives me a reason to live. Perhaps it's the way she wrinkles up her little button nose, and the humming to herself. Olivia used to do that, didn't she? Perhaps it's my imagination playing tricks. Her image is so faint in my head. When I close my eyes, I can only see a younger version of Sara.

I'm about to take a towel from the far wall where the water tap is, but my chain is too short and I don't want to wake Sara. Instead, I grab my t-shirt off the floor and use it to wipe my forehead, then my armpits, my back, my hair. Then I lay my duvet down on the soaked mattress and plant myself on top of it again. I let out a deep breath and stare at the ceiling while my body grows limp. It's pitch black, but there's no semblance of peace. The darkness and the silence in here must be like being trapped in one of those anechoic chambers, where you can even hear the sound of your own organs. I feel the beat of my heart, the blood flowing through me, and the remaining drips of sweat rolling down my body. It's killing me. I don't how long I lie like this, but eventually, my eyes finally close and allow me to find a slither of blank peace.

***

When I wake up again, I unpack the radio that Mal bought. It's an old silver thing, and smaller than my book. I pop in the batteries and power it up. Static fills the room. I extend the antenna and play around with the frequency. It's constant static whichever way I fumble with the frequency. *Damn it.* Nothing's ever easy in this place.

I stand up, raising the radio up and down, taking a few steps around the room whilst continuously changing the frequency, but nothing helps.

"You okay there?" Sara asks, watching me pace around.

"Yeah, just trying to get this thing to work," I answer her. "Signal isn't coming through down here."

I keep moving around the room and my frustration grows with every crackle of static from the old radio. I'm desperate to tune into a local station that might broadcast news about the disappearances. Just so I can get some peace of mind, knowing that they're still searching for us.

Sara watches me. "Maybe we're too deep underground," she says.

"Maybe," I concede, lowering the radio. "But I've got to try."

I find a spot near the corner of the room where the static seems a bit less aggressive and hoist the radio up high. I feel like some kind of makeshift astronaut trying to catch a signal from a distant star in the dark and empty vastness of space. For a second, there's a flicker of something—a fragment of a voice, a whiff of music—then it's gone, swallowed up by the static once more.

"You think it's broken?" Sara asks, getting up and coming closer.

I shake my head, refusing to give up. "No, it's just... tricky," I say. "These are old radios, you know. Like old dogs. They need the right kind of coaxing."

I twist the dial back and forth painstakingly, trying to find that elusive sweet spot. Sara squats beside me, invested in my struggle—our struggle. Together, we listen to the hisses and crackles, every tiny change in the sound making us hold our breath in anticipation.

Then, as if by magic, the static gives way to a clear, strong voice. It's a news anchor, talking about local events—mundane things that feel like a lifeline to the outside world.

Sara's face lights up, a genuine smile breaking through the gloom of our situation. "You did it!" she chimes.

I can't help but smile back, enjoying the foreign feeling of a small victory. "Quick, grab a stack of books to use as a stand!"

She grabs a handful of thick novels, dragging her chains across the floor. She places them on a neat tower while I hold up the radio, too scared to move an inch in case the voices disappear once more. After Sara is done with the book tower, I carefully place the radio on top of it and lean it against the wall. The voice of the news anchor remains stable.

We sit down together on the floor, the radio's voice filling the silence. It's a surreal feeling, hearing about traffic jams and weather forecasts, trivial things from a world we're no longer a part of. Even the most mundane topic suddenly interests me. Anything about the upstairs world, as Sara would call it, makes our little world seem so much bigger. She leans in closer, as if trying to absorb every word, every connection to normalcy. Then, the tone of the broadcast shifts. The anchor starts talking about ongoing police investigations. My heart races. Sara grips my hand. It's like the anchor is speaking directly to us.

"And in local news, authorities have discovered an abandoned truck off Route 50 near the old highway stretch," the anchor says. "The vehicle, identified as a freight truck, is believed to be linked to the recent string of disappearances in the area..."

Sara and I exchange a look filled with hope. "That's Midnight, my truck!" I say in astonishment. "They've found her!"

The anchor continues, "The truck, registered to one Hank Griffin, has sparked a renewed search effort in the area..."

Hank Griffin. My name, coming out of that radio! A sigh of relief escapes my lips. They're looking for us! That means there's still hope. We can't give up, not yet.

"But no leads have been found as of yet," the anchor adds. My heart sinks a bit, but I cling to the hope. They're close, they have to be.

Sara squeezes my hand tighter. "They're looking for you, Hank!" she says excitedly. "They might find us!"

I try to mask the turmoil inside me. "Yeah, they just might!"

We sit in silence, listening to the rest of the news, but my mind is racing. But there's also a gnawing fear. Mal. What if he hears this? What if he decides we're too much of a risk now? If he thinks the police are on to him, he might decide to get rid of us before we have a chance of escaping.

I glance at Sara. "We need to be ready," I whisper. "If they come looking, we might have to make a move."

Her jaw tightens in defiance. We both know that one wrong step could cost both our lives.

"Don't worry," I say. "We won't be here much longer."

"I know. When it's time, I'll be ready to fight. No more playing the nice little victim." She mimes a punching motion. It gives me strength to see she is willing to try. We share a laugh and, for a moment, our bleak existence doesn't matter because we have each other.

"He probably knows that we're not just going to submit to him without a fight, which is why he's playing nice right now, buying us things."

"He won't buy my obedience through DVDs and portable heaters," Sara says. "Good thing is that he seems to be becoming more and more trusting of us. We just need to play the part of his dutiful family."

I nod, grabbing one of the dinner knives and begin scraping it against the bottom of the wall in an attempt to sharpen the tip. "We'll have more options once he unchains us."

Above, the door to Mal's room above us slams shut. Both me and Sara raise our eyes towards the ceiling, listening to his footsteps, our smiles long gone. He's not alone. We hear a second pair of feet. I scramble to hide the knife underneath my mattress.

When our eyes come back down to look at each other, I can tell that we're thinking the same thing. Mal's next victim is close to joining us in the basement. I can't make out the words being spoken, but I hear a faint laugh. I think the stranger is a man, and I imagine them drinking up there. Mal reaching into his fridge, bringing out a couple of cold beers. Just like he did with me.

Sara gives up trying to eavesdrop. She sits down on her mattress and grabs a small jigsaw puzzle. "Wanna join me?" she asks. "Better than wondering what's happening up there."

"Sure," I say quietly and sit across from her. The top of the jigsaw puzzle box shows the finished design—a lush field filled with beautiful wildflowers. Vibrant hues of blue, green, yellow, and red. I can almost smell their scent in the soft, warm wind. Sara scatters the pieces in front of us and we start.

"Ever done one of these before?" I ask, breaking the silence as I fit two pieces together.

Sara looks up, a smile on her face. "Yeah, with my little brother. It was never my idea of fun, but we used to do them on rainy days."

"It's the small things that matter, right? You must miss him."

"Of course," she says, her face lighting up at the fond memories for a few seconds before she returns her focus on the puzzle. "What about you? Much of a puzzler?"

I chuckle softly. "I can't say I have done something like this ever. But I gotta admit, this is... calming, I guess."

We work together, slowly bringing the picture to life. Each piece feels like a small victory, a tiny step towards completing something, even if it's just a puzzle. It's an escape from the reality. Sara's much better at the puzzle than me. She quickly finds a piece that completes an entire section.

"Look, we're almost done with the top part," she points to the clear blue sky. "Sky is always the hardest."

I lean over to the section and our hands brush against each other's. We briefly look at each other and quickly pull away, returning to the puzzle. Her hand felt warm, familiar. I strike the thought from my mind.

"You know, when we get out of here," I begin, not entirely sure where I'm going with this. "I'd like to see a field like this. Just sit and watch the world go by."

Sara looks up, her eyes meeting mine. "I'd like that too," she says. "Maybe in California."

"Yeah, California," I say, more to myself than her. "Maybe I'll finally take a trip—"

"There!" Sara says cheerfully, placing the final piece. "We did it!"

I lean back, breaking out of my train of thought. Then I look down at the completed puzzle. "Looks great!"

"Looks beautiful!" Sara corrects me.

"We should do another one," I suggest, not ready to let go of this fleeting feeling of peace.

"I'd like that," Sara says, her smile broadening. "Do we have one that's more challenging?"

I look over the packages. "We've got two more," I say. "The big one is…" I read the description on the back, "called 'Nighthawks,' painted by Edward Hopper. And the other one is 'Garden at Sainte-Adresse' by Monet."

I pass both of the jigsaw puzzles to Sara to look over. She thinks for a moment, then decides on the Edward Hopper one. We take out the pieces. I read the full description on the back.

"One of the best-known images of twentieth-century art, the painting depicts an all-night diner in which three customers, all lost in their own thoughts, have congregated," I read out loud. I'm not sure if Sara has zoned out. "Shall I keep going?" I ask her. She nods in the affirmative, looking deep in thought rather than bored, so I pick up from where I left it. "Hopper's understanding of the expressive possibilities of light playing on simplified shapes gives the painting its beauty. Fluorescent lights had just come into use in the early 1940s, and the all-night diner emits an eerie glow, like a beacon on the dark street corner."

Just looking at the picture of the painting makes me feel a tinge of sadness and loneliness. I zone out for a while and get brought back to reality with the sound of a thud above. It startles me. Sara looks unshaken, though. She's already got around seven pieces of the new puzzle put together. With that, the hatch above us opens and Mal's jolly face peers in.

"Hiya, folks," he calls out to us. "Sorry for the ruckus upstairs. Me and a young fella were having a drink. You know him, Hank." He points to me. "The German hiker boy?"

I give him a silent nod, tensing with what I expect might follow.

"Be careful now, he's going to take a little tumble down the hatch!" Mal says cheerfully, as if he's delivering kegs of beer.

Suddenly, Sara pulls me by the hand and drags me away. She presses herself against the wall, knowing exactly what's about to happen. I follow her example and press myself against the wall, too. Sara shuts her eyes tightly. I'm about to whisper to her when the German hiker's body crashes down into the basement, landing on the concrete floor with a sickening thud. I hear a dozen bones cracking all at once, sending a shiver down my spine. The hiker looks lifeless, although I hear a faint groaning from him. Poor boy is still alive.

11

"What did you do to him?" I ask Mal as he descends the ladder.

"Just spiked his drink," Mal announces as if he did something really admirable. I feel sick just looking at the nonchalance in his face. Another family who will soon be missing a loved one. More innocent lives ruined.

"He'll be out for a while," Mal says, staring forebodingly at the young German boy's motionless body for a few seconds before wiping his palms and switching his gaze to me.

"Then again, maybe he won't wake up, who knows?" he announces, only looking at me, as if I'm guilty of something. I try to think about my brief encounter with the German hiker when I was having beers with this psychopath. I distinctly remember that I hadn't told him anything personal about me. It was Mal who asked questions about the places he had been, where he was from, and his favorite mountains. I remember being tired when the hiker arrived. All I had wanted was to leave the conversation and go to bed. So, why was Mal looking at me as if I had done something wrong? Was he trying to guilt-trip me for no reason? For just being there when the hiker arrived? I can't quite put my finger on what's going through Mal's head. Maybe he brought the hiker here because he had seen me and possibly seen my truck. *That's it.* They've both probably seen the news broadcast. I try to clear my head of all these thoughts and look away from Mal's eyes. But somehow, he holds my gaze.

"Hank, come here," he orders.

Stomach churning, I stand and take five steps towards him, keeping my guard up.

"This boy's heavy, so I'm going to need your help getting him through that door," Mal says casually, like we're discussing how to move an awkward wardrobe.

Out of the corner of my eye, Sara urges me to comply. This is exactly what we wanted, a glimpse into that room. Answers that will help our escape.

I wait for Mal to give me some instructions, but he just continues staring at me, as if it's a test. "How am I gonna help you when I'm shackled?" I point to the chain attached to the hook on the wall, hopeful that he'll set me free.

Mal steps towards me. I flinch, not sure what he's about to do. He stops in front of me and crouches. I half-expect him to pull out a knife and stab me or cut off an ear for being smart with him, but he takes a hold of his set of keys. "You better behave, Hank," Mal warns me. "Don't try anything funny."

I don't react. There are too many thoughts spiraling through my head. Although this was at the forefront of our plan all along, the fact that Mal's doing this still comes as a shock. I'm taller and probably stronger than him. Plus, this time I'm not drugged. I could take him down right now, beat him unconscious, set Sara free, and escape through the open hatch.

The conservative side of me ponders whether Mal still has that box cutter in his back pocket. Or something better that could change this whole thing around for the worse. I don't know if it's worth the risk. I can feel Sara's eyes burning into my back, like she knows what I'm thinking—I just wish I knew what she wanted me to do. My knife is still too dull to be of any use, so I can forget about that. And with Sara shackled, she wouldn't be much help if I was on the losing end of the fight.

Mal bends down and unlocks the chain. I glance over at Sara. She purses her lips and gives me a subtle shake of the head. Mal straightens himself and looks at me with a smile on his repulsive face. Although I'm unshackled, I don't feel any freer than before.

I rub my leg, trying to get the circulation back after being chained for so long. A strong urge to punch Mal's face and wipe the grin off it forever threatens to overcome me, but I fight it, reminding myself to stay patient this time. Sara seems to relax a little, dropping her shoulders after seeing that I wasn't about to do anything to get us killed.

"Right," Mal says, rubbing his palms together with glee. "That's done. Aren't you glad that I'm being such a good friend to you, Hank?"

"Yeah, I'm over the moon," I say, pretending to still be busy rubbing my leg.

"Well, let's move him, shall we?" Mal says to me impatiently, motioning towards the limp body of his latest victim.

I shuffle forward, doing as he asks. I hover over the unconscious hiker and bend down to lift his legs, while Mal grabs him under the arms. Mal counts to three and we lift him up. I don't expect him to be so heavy. My grip nearly slips as I lift him.

Sara watches us in silence, but she can barely look as we awkwardly maneuver the guy towards the ominous door. My weakened muscles strain under his weight. As we move, I keep an eye on Mal, trying to determine if he's carrying a concealed weapon on him, but I can't make out the telltale bulge.

Mal shuffles sideways, taking a hold of the boy's neck in a headlock, and dropping his arms. The fact that he had the strength to hold him up so easily takes me by surprise. With one arm now free, he reaches for his keys and unlocks the big metal door. He gives the door a push with one of his legs and it creaks open, revealing the room Sara and I have spent the last few days wondering about. It's dark, but I can make out the familiar silhouettes of various tools and objects that I can't yet place. Cold air seeps into my skin, making the hairs on my arms stand. The room is several degrees colder than our basement prison.

We lay the hiker down gently on the floor. The boy's breathing is shallow, and I fear he may not last much longer. Mal locks the door behind us, and for a moment, it's just the three of us in the room—the captor, the captive, and the latest unconscious victim. I think about Sara being alone on the other side of the door. I can't stand the idea of her being alone, so vulnerable. At least Mal's here with me, where he won't be able to hurt her.

"Good job, Hank," Mal says, patting me on the back as if we're old friends. It takes all my willpower not to recoil from his touch. "Thank you. Didn't know you'd be such a good sport!"

I look around, trying to absorb everything inside the room, anything that will aid me in escaping, but the light seeping in from the other room is not enough to pierce the darkness.

Mal flicks on a switch and a bright lamp overhead illuminates, revealing the room's contents. Several large freezers line the walls, their bulkiness casting shadows. A big metal table sits in the center of the room, like the prep tables in a restaurant kitchen. Its surface is stained and scratched—it's been well used.

An array of sharp knives, saws, and other tools adorn the wall, each meticulously arranged. It's like a butcher's shop. There are also various implements that I can't identify, each one looking more menacing than the last.

Mal notices me eyeing his stuff up. "Impressive, isn't it?" he asks me, gazing around with his chest puffed out. "It took me years to collect all these. They're my pride and joy." His voice is disturbingly casual, as if he's showing off something as mundane as a collection of rare postage stamps.

Surely, he can't be this stupid. All I need to do is grab one of those knives and it's over.

"You know, Hank, you could be very useful down here. You're strong and capable. We could be a great team, you and I."

The suggestion sends another chill down my spine. "Yeah, maybe," I say, playing along. Just need to catch him off guard and put an end to this nightmare.

"Great!" he says, pleased with my response. "I'll think of some tasks for you!"

I'm still struggling to understand what this place is. There are no other doorways here, just the massive freezers, tools, the table, and the same sort of water tap as in the other room.

Mal walks over to one of the freezers, opening it. I try looking over his shoulder to see what's inside, but he chuckles, seemingly amused by my reaction. "Curious?"

All I see inside is perfectly organized sets of steaks. Looks like several different kinds of cuts. I guess he really loves his meat. As he closes the freezer, I finally see the handle of a blade tucked in behind his jeans.

"Now, help me get him on the table," Mal says, as if it's the most normal thing in the world.

I follow his lead, grabbing him by his brown hiking boots whilst Mal hoists him up by the arms. Together, we throw him onto the table. I feel my stomach churn at the sickening slap the limp body makes as it slams onto the metal surface.

"Thanks, Hank," says Mal. "You're a champ. Now let's get you back. Freedom feels great, doesn't it?"

"What are you going to do with him?"

He smiles at me while leading me back towards the door. "Keep up the good behavior and perhaps I'll remove your shackle for good."

Freedom. This word lingers in my head. A scene plays out in my head—sprinting towards the wall of knives, grabbing hold of one in each hand. Smiling at the terrified look on Mal's face, creeping towards him, pushing the blades through his cold skin.

Mal leads me back to the other room, then bends down to chain me. I glance at Sara while he attaches the clasp to my leg. I can tell by her eyes that she's filled with questions about the room next door, but I can only offer her a solemn nod. We can talk when Mal is gone. I'm sure she's dying to know what's behind there, although I don't really know what to make of it myself.

Mal finishes locking my chain and straightens up. "Be good, guys," he says to us with a wink. "I'll join you both for a board game or two soon!" He waves and walks back into the cold room, shutting the door behind him.

"What did you see?" Sara asks, coming alive again the moment he's gone. "What's in there?"

I take a deep breath. "I don't really know. I mean, there's freezers for his meat, a bunch of tools, like knives, saws, others that I've never seen before. And a large metal table which the boy is lying on right now like a corpse in a mortuary, waiting for their damn autopsy."

Sara's face turns pale. "Hank. It's..."

"What?" I ask.

She tugs at the chain and scurries to the drain by the shower, spilling her guts out with a noise like a possessed spirit.

"Sara, what's wrong?"

She wipes her mouth with the back of her hand, her face filled with sheer disgust. "Don't you get it? It's a butchery! The meat he's been feeding us... it's human remains."

"No, it can't be." I don't want to believe it, but hearing her say it out loud suddenly makes perfect sense. "He's a fucking cannibal."

Sara's eyes brim with tears as she washes away her puke and settles back down on her mattress.

"It can't be." My head throbs again under the bandages. "He can't be that evil." I struggle to keep my composure, my mind racing with the gruesome reality of what happens in that room, where Mal dismembers his victims, where he turns people into mere objects for his sick desires, where he turns people into lumps of steak.

The door swings open, jolting me from my thoughts. Sara sits up straight. Mal's face peers in, his grin wide and unsettling.

"Time for a bit of learning, Hank!" he calls out to me so cheerfully that it sends chills down my spine. He walks towards me and unchains me once more with a jangle that echoes through the basement. Then he gestures for me to stand up.

I oblige, my legs stiff and unsteady. I don't know whether it's from sitting down or from the shock of seeing the butchery. Sara looks up at me, trying to hide the fear in them. Mal beckons for me to follow him back in. I let my feet drag me back into that nightmare of a room. I have no choice, like I'm on autopilot.

Once I walk through, Mal shuts the door behind me and locks it again. Now knowing what this room is really used for paints a different image in my head. The word *cannibal* repeats in my head over and over. I look down at the bite marks on my arm and hand. He wasn't just biting into me to defend himself, no. He was doing it to *taste* me. The revulsion I feel is like a thousand slugs crawling all over my body.

The German hiker now lies on the metal table fully naked. For a moment, I think he must be dead, but his chest is moving up and down. The sight of his helpless body knots my stomach.

"Now, Hank," Mal begins, a flicker of madness in his eyes. "Let's talk about the human body." He speaks with an eerie enthusiasm, gesturing vaguely at the hiker. "There's a lot to learn, but I promise it'll all be worth it. You need to know these things." His hands move above the hiker's body like a medical professional's.

I try to keep my composure, but inside, my mind is screaming. I glance at the hiker, then back at Mal, trying to decipher my next move, but I'm completely frozen and useless.

"Oh, before I forget," Mal says, rushing over to a cabinet next to the freezers in excitement. "Let's pop these on." He hands me a long white cotton coat, like the ones butchers wear. He puts on one himself, although his coat isn't so white anymore. It is stained with faint splashes of rusty brown, and it has clearly been washed many times over. Blood. They are splashes of blood that has been washed and bleached. I feel paralyzed, as though Mal has taken a hold over me, and wrestled control of my spirit.

"Let's go over what to avoid, shall we?" Mal says, taking a scalpel off the metal tray. "I made these mistakes so you won't have to." He laughs. Thank God Sara is not here. I might just be able to survive this. But Sara? No chance.

Mal points to the hiker's fingers with the sharp edge of his scalpel. "These little fellas, trust me, are not worth it," he says. "You'd think they'd be crispy like chicken feet, and great with beer, right? But no." He takes the scalpel and slices the hiker's index finger, making a deep incision all around the flesh. Blood oozes out, flowing over his hand, and begins to drip down the edge of the table.

I nearly fall as my feet shuffle me back, desperate to put distance between myself and the horrific sight.

"It's okay, Hank," he says, leering at me. "It's your first time. I don't expect you to react any differently. Just make sure you listen and learn, okay?"

He grips the cut finger and tugs at the flesh like a dog pulling a chew toy. It takes several efforts before the skin comes off and all that remains is the bony finger covered in a layer of slimy residue. Mal holds the skin in the palm of his hands and squishes it with his thumb and index finger as though he's playing with a piece of rubber, then slaps it down on the floor away from us. My stomach churns once again and bile rises in my throat.

"Do we eat the fingers?" Mal asks me.

"N-no." I shake my head with unease, frozen against the wall, scared that I might throw up any second.

"That's right," says Mal, like a proud professor teaching an anatomy class for cannibals. "Next, the ears." He squats down and stares into the boy's ear canal.

"Hello, can anyone hear me?" Mal laughs to himself, then looks at me. "Don't worry, I've administered a strong anesthetic. He's out. Won't feel any pain." He looks up at the ceiling. "At least, I don't *think* so anyway."

All I can do is nod. I really hope the boy doesn't feel a thing. I eye the tools behind him, desperately calculating my chances of running past him to grab a knife before he has a chance to take out his. They seem slim-to-nonexistent. I decide to remain a spectator for a little longer and take a few steps closer to the table.

"Glad to see you're eager to learn," says Mal. Using the same scalpel, he slices cleanly through the hiker's ear and holds it up high, examining it in the light before biting down on it a few times. "Chewy but kinda tasty," he announces. "I suggest not to waste your time with them." He chucks it aside. A steady but continuous flow of blood runs down the boy's neck. The tiled floor below us is slowly turning from a bleak grey to a smeared ruby red.

"Now, onto the good stuff." Mal wipes his mouth with the sleeve of his shirt and smiles, baring his blood-stained teeth while looking at the hiker's body. "What do we like to eat? Liver, brain, tongue is a hit-or-miss, ribs, neck, butt, thighs... But let's not get ahead of ourselves." He licks his dry lips, giving me the impression that he's salivating just thinking about it all.

Then he looks at me, making me flinch. "Which part of him would you like to eat for dinner, Hank?"

I clear my throat, unsure what to say. The scalpel glistens in Mal's hand. I have to answer, or his scalpel could be drawing my blood next.

"Speak up," Mal says. This time, his voice is less gentle.

"I don't eat human meat, Mal."

"Oh, come on, Hank, don't lie to yourself. Didn't hear any complaints the other day."

My mouth opens and closes, but words don't come out. Mal starts fidgeting and tapping his foot. Before I can summon a response, he pulls open the mouth of the hiker, yanks the tongue between forefinger and thumb, and slices it cleanly off. I turn away as a tiny blot of vomit rises in my mouth and I have to swallow it, burning my throat.

"Look at me, Hank!" Mal commands me in a dangerous voice. "Don't you dare look away!"

I turn to face him again, staring in disgust.

He takes the tongue dripping with blood and jams it into his mouth. Red flows down the sides of his mouth whilst he chews. The boy's mouth fills like an overflowing bath and he begins to choke on the blood. Seconds later, his body goes into shock, his entire body spasming, edging closer to the side of the table.

Mal takes several heavy steps towards the wall, grabs a long and extremely sharp looking knife. Using both hands, he stabs it into the boy's chest, right through the heart. The boy's spasming body jerks several times, then falls still while air gurgles from his blood-filled mouth.

My heart is racing. Everything seems unreal, a waking nightmare where I have just witnessed a cold-blooded murder. There is blood everywhere, even on my white coat, on the walls, on the floor. How on earth do you clean up this much mess?

"What part would you like to eat?" Mal asks again calmly whilst throwing the bloody knife into the sink, where it lands with a clatter. He returns to the body and runs his hand along the torso and down the thigh as if appraising the quality of a butchered lamb.

Fuck this.

While his back is turned, I sprint towards the wall, grabbing a massive cleaver knife in one hand and a carving knife in the other. He turns to me, seemingly unphased as he washes his hands.

"Can't make up your mind which to use? Oh, Hank. You're a real joker. Put the knives down."

I think about rushing him like I had imagined, but I can't afford to make another mistake. "You can't do this to people. It's not right."

"I like you, Hank. You've got spunk. That's exactly why you're the perfect third addition to our family."

143

"What family!? We're not your family, Mal. I don't know what the hell is going on in that head of yours, but if you don't give me your keys right now, I'm going to take them off you by force."

My pathetic little speech only seems to make him excited. As he exhales into the cold room, a misty cloud travels towards me.

"Ooh, Hank, you really know how to keep the days down here exciting, don't you?" He says, taking a hold of the knife he had placed in the sink. He takes a series of short steps towards me with the knife pointed down, blood still dripping onto the floor.

"Don't come any closer," I say, gripping both knives tighter and brandishing them towards him.

"I don't mind a little scuffle, Hank. Chaos is in our nature, after all." Mal says it so calmly, as though we're not seconds away from a potential fight to the death. He shoots me a smile and runs right at me, swinging wildly.

I take a few steps to the side and slice through the air with the cleaver, knocking his blade away. With the carving knife, I lunge forward, clipping Mal's side. But he's still coming at me. Before I can make my next move, his fist comes flying at me, connecting with my jaw.

I stumble back, dropping the heavy cleaver, but holding on to the second knife. He rushes towards me like a rabid animal, pouncing on me before I even have a chance to stand. I'm too slow. He grabs my wrist, then tries head-butting me. I turn my head just in time to avoid getting my nose splattered across my face, but his head still smashes into my cheekbone.

With Mal's entire weight on me, I'm pinned against the blood-drenched floor. I keep a firm hold on my remaining knife, but with his arm on my wrist, I can't do anything. I swing with my free arm, landing three shots into the side of his head and neck, but he won't budge, and now he's eyeing the cleaver behind us.

He hisses at me and scurries away towards it whilst I push myself in the opposite direction and stand up, my shoes slipping against the slick floor. Mal feels the side of his torso where I cut him, and his hand comes away covered in his own blood. He doesn't look phased by it, and his expression is more one of curiosity.

"That stings, Hank." he says calmly. "You'll really wish you hadn't cut me."

I use the opportunity to grab something from the wall. I think about throwing knives at him, but that could easily backfire, so I grab a claw hammer instead. It's got some weight to it—I just need one clean shot to his head and he'll be out cold.

"Come on, you fucker!" I scream, charging at him with one arm back, ready to swing the hammer.

He flashes me a bloody smile. Just as I swing forward, he dashes to the side so wildly that he slips. While he flings his arm out for balance, I swing my other arm sideways with the carving knife towards him, but he dodges and counters with lightning speed. Before I know it, the massive cleaver swoops down. In a desperate attempt to block it, I lift my hammer, but he's got too much power behind it. The cleaver clangs into the hammer head and scrapes down the rubber grip until it buries itself inside my hand. A jolt of electricity shoots through my fingers and up to my arm.

I scream as blood gushes out all over the floor tiles and I collapse to my knees. Amidst the pool of red, my nail-less ring finger and pinkie lay like two discarded chipolatas. I drop my knife and grab my wounded hand. The smashed bones peek through, severed an inch above the knuckle.

When I look up again, Mal dashes towards me from the metal cart on the other side of the room with a syringe in his hand. I try to stand, but he tackles me into a wall. I groan, jabbing him in his ribs multiple times with my able arm, but he's too strong. Mal wraps his arms around my torso, trying to bring me down to the floor, but I keep my feet firmly planted on the ground and continue delivering punches. This time, my fists connect with the sides of his head, but it seems to do no damage.

With a wild roar, he picks me up and slams me down on the ground. I land right on my tailbone. *Fuck, that hurts.* He bares his teeth as though he's preparing to bite me. I hurl my fist at his mouth, knocking him backwards, spewing blood all over my hand and the floor.

The punch buys enough time to get back on my feet, but as soon as I do, I'm overcome by dizziness. I'm surrounded by a pool of my own blood. The whole world becomes a blur, and I forget that I'm fighting a battle for life and death.

Mal maneuvers around me before I can react and I feel a sting in my buttock. My body goes into autopilot, and I swing my arms at him, but he's already retreated to the other side of the room and the blows hit nothing but thin air.

I try stepping towards him, but skid on a pool of blood. Who knows whether it's mine, Mal's, or the hitchhiker's? Perhaps all three. I land hard, knocking the wind from my chest. I ease shallow breaths into my lungs and sit up. Mal is bent over, rummaging through a compartment under the sink. Blood jets from the stumps of my missing fingers. I squeeze the wrist to slow the bleeding, but it's futile and I need a tourniquet urgently. Now, the pain comes. Excruciating pain that sends me into a screaming frenzy. I've never felt pain like this before.

Mal comes back with rope, but I'm not ready to give in, not yet. I hurl myself into him, knocking him over, and pummel him with punches from my good hand. When he grips my wrists, I result to using my teeth, sinking my mouth deeply into his neck. I pull left and right, ripping away some of his skin and flesh before spitting it out.

Mal screams. For the first time, he looks frightened. He wriggles himself away, both hands squeezing down on his gaping wound.

I take the opportunity to yank his keys, ripping them off his belt loop. I push open the heavy door and try to run back through to the main room, but this quickly turns into a slow crawl as my legs give out.

"Hank? What happened?" Sara's mouth is wide open. I must look like an apparition of horror.

"Take the keys!" I shout, throwing them across to her.

Sara grabs them, staining her hands red. She stretches her leg out, turning the metal clasp so that the keyhole faces her. She tries the first key, but it doesn't fit. Then another, but it just won't unlock her leg clasp.

I hear Mal's voice moan from the room of death behind me.

"Why aren't these damn keys working!?" she shouts, nostrils flaring in panic. The last key does the trick, and Sara frees herself then runs towards me. "Oh my god, your hand!" Her face wrinkles in horror as she sees the missing fingers.

"I'm okay. Just get up that ladder and unlock the hatch. Quickly now."

Sara stands on tiptoes, inserting a key into the hatch and unlocking it. With a push, the hatch door swings up and brings us one step closer to freedom.

"Come on, Hank," she gestures for me to climb up.

I pull myself to the ladder, but my legs are completely numb. I can't stand up, and I don't have the strength to pull myself. "Just go," I urge her. "Leave me and get help."

Reluctantly, she climbs to the top and pulls herself up the hatch, into Mal's room. She drops the set of keys down to me, telling me to lock the door to the butchery. I keep a firm hold over my fingers to stop the bleeding. We've done it. Help will be here soon.

As I slowly crawl my way to the metal door, clinching onto the keys, Sara's voice echoes down.

"It's fucking double-locked," she says, pounding on the front door. "I need the keys."

Before I can turn to make my way back towards the ladder, I feel a heavy weight on my back. Mal steps over me and claws his way up the ladder.

I'm powerless, unable to help. I clench my fist in desperation, but I know I cannot stop him. I can't feel my legs, and my body's going cold. Everything's beginning to blur, even Sara's voice when she screams at the top of her lungs, and the sounds of slamming against the floorboards above me, followed by a slapping that quickly fades into silence.

"Get back down," I hear Mal's calm voice call out, followed by Sara making her way down the ladder, shaking all over. Just as she gets halfway down, Mal kicks her in the head. She plummets down onto the hard floor, smacking her head. She groans, lies still, then doesn't make a sound.

"You fucking animal," I curse out at him, feeling the blow worse than my own pain.

He climbs down, locking the hatch on the way. "I could say the same about you. Very...bitey," he chuckles, before groaning as he feels his neck wound.

12

I must have passed out, because I find myself sitting on a chair in the butchery room with my hands tied. My right hand is bandaged up, but the pain has not decreased. The whole hand throbs with the jerking rhythm of my heart.

"Good, you're awake."

The left side of Mal's neck is covered with a wound dressing. I smile, seeing his battered face. Looks like I've been out for a while, because he's dressed in a clean change of clothes, without a smidge of blood on him. Looking down at myself, I realize that I'm no longer covered in blood, either.

"I took the liberty of washing you. You looked hideous. But my god you're heavy," Mal says, smiling.

"Where's Sara?" I ask.

"She's fine, just sleeping. She hit her head pretty hard on her way down, so she needs her rest."

I try moving my legs, but they won't budge. "What did you do to me?"

"Don't worry, it's just a numbing agent. It'll wear off. Probably in a few hours, I guess." He takes a few steps towards me and bends down. "I was too optimistic about you acclimatizing to your new home quickly. I'll admit my fault there. But on the bright side, wasn't that fun? I felt so alive!"

I don't respond.

"Anyway, where were we?" he asks, turning to the dead hiker on the table. "Ah yes. Which part are you having for dinner?"

I refuse to play his game. I'm not a cannibal, and I'd rather die than give in.

His face twitches as he steps towards me. "Speak," he says, spittle landing on my face.

"No."

He lets out a frustrated grunt and fetches one of his tools. I try to see which one but can't rotate my neck far enough, although I probably don't want to know.

"I'm going to give you one last chance," he says, holding up a power saw to my eye. With the flick of a switch, it roars to life. I swallow my breath, holding my body as still as a statue. Inches in front of my face, the metal strip lined with teeth rotates back and forth.

"Thigh." The word just spouts out without my permission. My body is so desperate to survive that it no longer cares about such luxuries as a moral compass.

Mal gives me a nod of approval and buries the blade into the hiker's meaty quads. It quickly digs through the flesh but jerks back as it hits bone with a grinding noise. It takes several attempts to get through. The leg, amputated six inches below the groin, thuds to the floor and Mal puts down the blade and holds up his bounty. I try looking away, but Mal makes me watch him skin the leg, slapping my face every time I turn away.

"I'm not usually this sloppy, Hank, do forgive me," he tells me. "Perhaps I'm a little tired from our play time earlier. Plus, I'd usually make sure that the prey has no food for forty-eight hours, but plenty of water. The fasting helps flush the system, purging toxins and waste, as well as making bleeding and cleaning easier. But the guy wouldn't stop talking. I really don't think you'd have been able to handle his blabber, either." Some blood squirts onto Mal's face, which he immediately wipes but ends up just smudging it over a large portion of his face.

He then walks behind me and pushes my chair. I squint at the screeching of the chair legs against the floor until I'm next to the table.

"Touch him," Mal instructs. With a grunt, he flips the hiker around onto his stomach. His strength is impressive.

I grudgingly agree, holding my breath as soon as the tip of my finger touches the cold body. It's already stiffening, and the skin is changing color from a milky pale to a bluish hue. I lean back into my chair and watch Mal grab a large hook from his impressive wall of tools. It looks like a gigantic version of a fishing hook, the sort of implement that a butcher would use to hang an animal to bleed it out.

Using all his force, Mal stabs the hook into the boy's shoulder, then pushes it through even deeper with a gruesome crunching sound that makes me retch. He repeats the process with a second hook on the other shoulder, and attaches the hooks to a chain, which he then hoists up using a lever. The chains squeak and the body rises from the table, jerking like a puppet on strings, blood still spurting out from the hole in the boy's ear and his dismembered finger, as well as the stump of his leg. I can now see the bone sticking out of the flesh. Without hesitation, Mal slices directly down the boy's stomach, letting his organs flop out onto the floor with a disgusting slithery slap. The coppery stench of shit fills the room, and this time I can't hold the vomit and it spews from my mouth.

"You can go now," Mal tells me softly, continuing to dismember the body. He slices at the boy's neck, taking off the head, but instead of rolling down, I see it is still clinging on by a thick, rubbery tendon. He leaves it hanging and instead goes to work on the arms with more surgical precision.

I try to do as he commands, but when I try to get up, my legs give out and I find myself back on the floor like a drunk who cannot get up.

Mal's hysterical laughter spills from across the room. "Oh Hank, you're such a character. Come on now, get the fuck out of the room."

Gritting my teeth, I crawl my way out, shutting the door behind me. I lean against the door and hang my head, sucking in gusts of air, yet it feels like I can't get any oxygen into my lungs. My heart is racing like never before. I hear Sara's voice echoing as if she is calling out to me in a dream, but my ears and brain can no longer work in tandem to decipher the words. My head is spinning. All I can think of is that I need to wash off this awful sin from my body. It disgusts me. Nothing will ever be the same.

I rip the clothes off my body, forgetting that Sara is here—or perhaps no longer caring—then chuck them down on the floor and run to the makeshift shower, where I twist the taps as quickly as possible, letting the ice-cold water hit my legs before it even warms up.

I'm shaking all over and my teeth are clattering. Why did Mal make me go through that? The picture of the boy's dismembered body sends a vile liquid up my throat once more. I throw up all over myself, but the water quickly washes it down the drain. If only my shame would come off so easily.

13

It's dinnertime. What can I say? The tearing of the boy's flesh still haunts me. I'm back where I started—my leg chained to the wall, watching Mal take bite after bite of the perfectly cooked meat. While he chews ravenously, I remind myself what he is really eating. I'm starving but there's no way in hell I'm eating that, and nothing he says will change my mind. Sara doesn't take a bite either, knowing for certain now the grim truth she surely suspected. She lifts her arm up every couple of minutes to check the bump on her head—she must have bashed herself pretty hard.

A thought goes through my mind—with us having eaten *it,* have we damned ourselves? I doubt God looks favorably on cannibals. The thought of not seeing Sally in the afterlife sends a jolting pain through my chest. Could she ever forgive me? Can God?

Mal doesn't say a word during his dinner. He just sits there, savoring each morsel, licking his lips between bites. Once he's finished with his steak, he watches me with an unsettling intensity. He leans forward, his elbows resting on the table, with a strange fervor in his eyes.

"You know, Hank," he starts, his voice taking on a tone that's eerily calm and collected. "There's more to this than just survival or indulgence."

A chill crawls up my spine. "What do you mean?" I ask, although I'm not sure whether I want to hear his answer.

Mal's eyes seem to glint in the dim light of the basement. "Eating this meat, I mean. It's a sacred act, you know. It brings us closer to God."

"Closer to God?" I repeat in astonishment. "How in the world does eating a person do that?"

Mal smiles, but it's not a comforting expression. "Just like the bread and wine in church, Hank. They represent the body and blood of the Christ, right? Well, this," he gestures to the meat on my plate, "this is my communion."

"That's blasphemy," I mutter. Sara just sits back and puts her head in between her knees and sobs gently. Both our plates are untouched.

Mal chuckles, unfazed by my admonishment. "To you, maybe," he says with a casual shrug like I'd criticized his choice of music rather than his moral code. "But to me, it's a profound truth. When I consume someone, I'm not just eating their meat, delicious as it is. I'm taking in their essence, their spirit. It's a form of worship, and a way to connect with the divine."

I shake my head in disbelief. "That's pretty twisted, Mal. It's not worship, it's murder. Cold-blooded murder."

Mal leans back, his expression pensive as though he's keen to get into a debate. "Is it?" he asks, his eyes steady on mine. "Think about it, Hank. All throughout history, sacrifices have been made in the name of religion. How is this any different?"

"Because those were animals, not people," I argue.

"That's not true," Mal says, shaking his head. "Plenty of civilizations sacrificed people to please their Gods. The Inca, Greeks, Romans, want me to go on?"

I shake my head in disagreement. "Well, they were all primitive," I say finally. In truth, I know nothing about history, so I'm fighting a losing battle here.

"Come on, Hank, don't try to fool yourself!" Mal chuckles. "They were smarter than us in many ways. Just look at all the stuff they invented. And who's to say that one life is more valuable than another? We all return to the earth in the end. In consuming them, I honor their existence."

"Honor?" I retort, feeling a surge of revulsion. "You call this honor? It's sacrilege."

"Yes, I call this honor," Mal insists, his voice growing more animated. "Each person I've chosen, they've become a part of me, a part of my journey to enlightenment. I remember every single one of them. Their stories, their fears, their hopes. In a way, they live on through me. A greater part of something bigger than any of us."

Sara, who has been silent this whole time, finally speaks up, her voice barely above a whisper. "But they didn't choose this. You took away their ability to choose when you killed them."

Mal's gaze softens as he looks at her. "I know it's hard to understand, Sara," he says gently. "But believe me, what I do, I do with the utmost respect and care. They're not just meat. They're sacred offerings."

I can't help but scoff. *Sacred offerings? You're delusional.* I want to say it out loud, but I control myself. I don't want to lose any more fingers tonight.

Mal shakes his head, a sad smile on his face. "I don't expect you two to understand, not yet. It's not something everyone can comprehend. But in time, you might see the truth in my words."

"And what truth is that?" I ask.

"That in embracing what society fears and condemns, we can find a deeper connection to the world around us," Mal explains. "A deeper connection to the divine force that guides us all."

I can't tell if this is a heated discussion or just a debate, but Mal doesn't seem one bit upset.

"Sara," Mal says. "Be a dear and wash the dishes up. I'm sorry if the steak wasn't to your liking today. I tried my best to cook it with love. Put the meat in a bag and I'll leave it outside for the animals. Nothing goes to waste here. Circle of life, and all that."

She nods and takes our plates, knives and forks, empties the meat into a bag that Mal gave her, doing well to hide her disgust, before walking away to wash them under the tap we use for showering. After our near escape, I imagine that she's overthinking what Mal might do to us, but I'm starting to think that he can't imagine a life without our company. Why else would he keep me alive after my escape attempt?

"Hank, I'm really glad that you feel comfortable enough to debate me and give me your opinion," Mal says. "I certainly don't want you to feel you have to agree with everything I say or do from the outset. You're your own person. Clearly, you're strong-willed. You showed me that today."

I burst out laughing. Not because I find anything funny, just the ridiculousness of it all. I look like something out of a horror movie, with the amount of gashes and bruises I'm bearing. Unable to help myself, I thank him with no small hint of sarcasm, inwardly scoffing at the irony in his words.

"Here, I was going to hand this over earlier," Mal hands me a fresh pack of cigarettes. "In exchange for a little more conversation."

I've been dying for a cig since I got here, but I don't give him the satisfaction. I just give him a nod and take the pack. What kind of conversation does he want to have, anyway?

Mal gestures with his head to the vent on the wall above our mattresses. "Let's smoke here," he says to me. "Don't want to blow smoke towards Sara, though."

Sara takes the hint and tries stepping away to the other side of the room, but the chain around her ankle stops her before she makes it halfway. "It's not long enough," she says.

He gives her this calculating look, as though he's weighing out the chances of her trying something stupid. After seeing the defeat in her face, he unshackles her ankle, letting her free.

Sara gives me a sheepish look as she walks off, her eyes begging me to submit. Perhaps Mal has finally broken her spirit. No wonder, after two failed escape attempts, not to mention the physical and psychological pain we've endured.

We stand by the vent, and Mal lights his cigarette and leans against the wall, watching the smoke curl up and disappear. The old metal vent groans slightly as the smoke gets sucked away. When he hands me the lighter, I light mine up and take a deep drag, feeling the nicotine hit my system, welcoming it like a long-lost friend. Mal doesn't ask for the lighter back, so I keep hold of it, my fist clenched tight.

"So, Hank," Mal begins, his tone casual. "I know it's been hard for you to adjust to life here, in your new home. So, no hard feelings about earlier?"

"Thanks," I say gruffly.

Mal nods away, puffing on his cigarette.

"I know you value your freedom, your *you* time," he goes on. "So, I'll give you some time to yourself for a while. I need to go somewhere, anyway."

I take another drag, feeling a little more at ease with the euphoria of a nicotine rush massaging my tingling scalp. The smoke creates a barrier between us, a thin veil of normalcy in this twisted situation. "Where to?"

"My church."

I flick the ash off my cigarette, waiting for him to continue.

"At first, this place was just built to be a survival bunker for an apocalypse-type event. Although money dried up halfway through the project, so it's not quite finished yet. But anyway, when I found the Church, I realized a bigger vision for the place. That's when I started bringing people over about a year back."

"So, what's this church all about?" I ask, but it comes out more aggressive that I'd planned. I guess I can't stop my mind from lashing out.

"Church of Euthanasia," Mal says, quieter than before. "We're all about saving Mother Nature."

"Like, planting trees?"

Mal nearly chokes on cigarette smoke, seeming to find my question amusing. "No, not like that. Suicide. We see it as an act of self-sacrifice for the planet. Abortion, non-procreative sexual acts and cannibalism as a method to control the human population. Extreme, I know, but the situation we're in as a species demands an extreme response."

"That's one hell of a church. And you lay that all out publicly? Don't think the law looks favorably on cannibals and killers."

"Well, not exactly. There's a loophole we use," Mal chuckles. "In forty-nine of the fifty states, cannibalism isn't actually illegal. The church can't say, 'hey, everyone, go round and kill people so that you can eat them,' but we can advertise the fact we endorse eating human meat without actually breaking any laws."

"So, everyone at the church is a murderer?" I ask.

"To be honest, I don't know anyone else who has taken a life for the cause," Mal says with a shrug. "They mostly buy the bodies of people that are already dead. It's easier to get a hold of them than you think."

"So, why don't you do that?" I ask. "Why do you kill?"

He takes a moment to think. "Well, I guess I just like the thrill," he says after a few seconds. "It's... different."

"And where is this church?" I intend to gather every piece of information I can about him, so that the police can catch every other fucker associated with him once we're out of here. All his evil friends can rot in jail as accomplices, too, for all I care.

"It's not a place you'd find on a map," Mal says with a slight smile. "It's in the woods. Far away from this town. From any town."

I nod away, hoping Mal will continue. Soon, he does. "I believe we're overpopulating the planet. We are destroying it. The Church's teachings make sense to me. It's about balance, about taking responsibility for our actions. I see my work here as part of that. And when it's my time, I'll follow the path laid out by the Church.

14

Mal has been gone for two days now, I think. It's hard to keep track of time with no light and no visitors. My mental sharpness is returning, and the pain from my battle with Mal has subsided to a manageable throb. With both me and Sara unshackled, I can think more clearly. My body's less tense too.

While he's gone, me and Sara continue planning our escape. But nothing seems plausible with the overhead hatch locked from the outside. We take turns to bash at it with anything we can find—fists, shower head, makeshift blade. Even tried burning it with the lighter I took from Mal. Nothing comes close.

The door to the butchery is unlocked, although I don't dare to step inside, knowing that the hiker kid's body is hung up by the flesh. I went in once to check if he'd been dumb enough to leave all his tools there, but most of the heavy-duty stuff has gone. There's nothing we can use to escape.

Sara kept herself busy with the puzzles for a while, although, after doing the same ones over and over, she snapped, releasing the pent-up rage into the cardboard puzzle boxes, pummeling them flat with her dainty fists.

The image of the butchery behind the closed door and the knowledge that I have committed an act of cannibalism haunt me, but I try pushing the thoughts from my mind. I remind myself that I didn't know what I was eating. It's my defense. To myself, to Sally, to God, and to anyone who will listen.

Our store-bought food ran dry after the first day. There's nothing left, not even the crumbs from the sandwiches. We spent an entire hour this morning, like pathetic, scared little mice, scavenging for even the smallest fragments.

"I'm hungry," Sara complains, standing up from her bed. "Is there anything left?"

I shake my head. "We'll just have to hold out, I suppose."

"When do you think he's coming back?"

I shake my head again. "My best guess is any day now. His church can't be that far away."

The truth of my suspicions, I keep to myself. I reckon that this is all a part of Mal's ingenious plan. Leaving us here for days with nothing to eat. He knows we're going to starve. And the only source of food is through *that* door. He may have taken most of the tools, but he left enough for us to feed ourselves, if we get desperate enough.

Now that both me and Sara know what he's been feeding us, he understands we won't willingly eat what he cooks for us, so he's left us here to make a conscious choice—eat the meat or die.

Sara puts her hand on my shoulder. "You okay, Hank?"

"Yeah," I say, unconvincingly.

"You're worried about the food, right?"

I nod.

"Don't worry," Sara says. "Mal will be back soon. He's never been gone for more than a few days at a time."

"I've got a bad feeling," I say as I point to the shut door. I have to tell her. "That's where he keeps them. The meat. The victims. All of them. In massive freezers. And that boy, he's strung up by a great big hook like a gutted fish on the other side of that door."

I'm sure she already had a good idea of what's behind the door. But hearing this, Sara covers her mouth with both hands. The sudden visualization must have struck her with its full force.

"All the freezers are locked with a padlock," I continue. "I can't open them without his keys, but we both know what's inside of them."

Sara listens to me with her hands clasped over her mouth, her eyes wide.

"Mal just left the boy there hanging like he's an animal. His blood and guts are still all over the floor. And I don't think that he left him there by coincidence. Mal is clinical, methodical. He knows that the body will start decaying and leaving a stench. My hunch is that it's a test. He wants us to be self-sufficient, to help him with his work. To submit to his vile way of life."

Sara shakes her head over and over, grabbing at her hair. "No! I'm not eating any more of it! I can't! In fact, I'd rather starve to death!"

This whole time, I thought she was handling the whole cannibalism thing better than me, but now I see she was just keeping all her repulsion hidden deep inside. I step towards her and wrap my arms around her, feeling her delicate skin against mine. She accepts my hug and clings to me, sobbing.

"Shh, it's okay," I tell her, stroking her hair. "We won't give in. He doesn't deserve the satisfaction."

Sara nods, her face planted in my chest.

"We can make it at least a week without food," I say, although I'm not actually sure. "We have plenty of water, so we can at least stay hydrated. Let's hold out, okay?"

"I can't stand it anymore," Sara wails. "We need to escape while he's gone. Calling him Daddy, sitting up straight. I can't put on the act anymore. I just want to go home."

She wraps herself around me even tighter. Her nails dig into me, and her warm tears soak through my shirt.

I try to calm her, despite the strange sensations running through my body. "We're in this together and we'll get out together too, alright? I won't let Mal hurt you. I promise."

15

By my best estimate, at least five days have passed without a sign of Mal, but trust me, it feels like twenty. My stomach cries out non-stop, begging for me to shove some food down my throat. My mind's even trying to convince me to grab anything—the dust off the floor, the cardboard boxes from our boardgames.

Sara seems worse off than me, though. She's smaller, skinnier. I see her clutching onto her stomach all day, walking around the perimeter of the basement in circles, moaning softly.

The starvation makes me constantly nauseous. Stomach acid keeps traveling up my throat several times throughout the day, and I have no choice but to throw up. The bile tastes foul and burns the lining of my throat. Its color a bright, unhealthy yellow. Having no energy left is an understatement. I physically and mentally don't have the capability to have a conversation with Sara, and neither does she. We lack the strength even to open our mouths.

Yet another day clocks in without signaling Mal's return. Halfway through the day, my appetite disappears almost entirely. My skin is clammy and feverish, my heart skittering, and I start to panic. I remember watching a documentary sometime back. It said that when you starve yourself to the brink of death, your stomach acids start to eat your body from the inside. I keep thinking about it—my stomach acids gnawing at my flesh, the possibility of me bleeding to death from inside.

I'm probably overthinking. I frequently picture myself coughing up and vomiting blood. The vivid picture brings back memories of the German hiker being gutted like a fish. My stomach growls and churns, while an excruciating pain burns inside me; a fire that can never be extinguished. I am a cannibal, and I have consumed another human being.

I'm colder than usual. Biology or science was never a strength, but my guess is it's because my body is low on fat. I don't know, but I can feel my ribs like when I was a skinny little runt at nine or ten. It doesn't help that our little heater broke two days ago.

Sara looks at me as I shiver and gives me a sympathetic look. "Cold?" she asks, curled up in her corner. It's more of a statement than a question, but I nod in agreement and smile at her weakly. She hasn't moved much in the last three days, except to go to the toilet. I don't know how she survives. My body is shutting down, or rather, prioritizing itself to focus on other things, such as staying sane—perhaps not the smartest idea when insanity seems preferable. I drink more and more water with every passing hour, to the point where it makes me want to throw up. Hopefully, the water will at least dilute the acidity in my stomach and stop it from eating itself from the inside. I'm so empty that the liquid flows right through me, and I urinate at least ten times a day. It stinks of something I cannot place. And on top of that, no matter how much we sleep, we cannot prevent exhaustion from taking over.

Our efforts to escape have ground to a halt.

***

It's been around seven or eight days without Mal here. I've lost count, but definitely a week or more. Sara hasn't moved from her spot in the corner for at least twenty-four hours, not even to use the toilet. I don't think she's even drank any water. She's not speaking to me anymore, either. Not one word. Not that I have the strength left in my body to talk much. I also think the non-moving, non-speaking approach is the best way to conserve our energy. My mind and body are begging me to do something, anything. They tell me I won't last much longer on water alone. Death is a constant specter in the distance, but growing closer and closer each day. How long until it arrives to claim one of us? The other will surely succumb soon after.

As Mal's image lingers in my mind, rage builds up inside me. The thought of him wanting me to walk into that butchery and cut up the German boy. To eat him, to survive. If I had the strength, I'd punch a wall right now. Or better yet, have Mal climb down here right now so I can strangle him. Better use of energy than cutting up that decaying body for food. *Food.* Those words echo through my mind. The last day, the hunger has returned with a vengeance. In comparison, the previous sensations were mild pangs.

"Sara," I call out, standing up. "I'll be back soon, okay?"

She doesn't respond. I'm sure she knows what I'm implying. We've put it off long enough. Sara's strong-willed, but I know that we'll both die if we let our morals come before survival. My eyes are set on the shut door to Mal's butchery as I walk over to it.

I stop in front of it and take a deep breath. As I pull the door open, a strong whiff of decaying matter sends me stumbling back in a coughing fit, gagging. I completely forgot that the boy's body was still hung up. After slamming the door shut again, I cover my mouth and beg myself not to throw up all over the floor, not that I have anything in my stomach except liquid. The stench has crawled its way up my nose. It's so distinct, with a hint of what I can only describe as sweet but decayed fruit.

From huge, hollow sockets, Sara stares at me with empty, lifeless eyes. I don't think the stink has reached her nose. Or if it has, she just doesn't have any energy left in her body to react.

With my hand on the cold door handle, I take a deep breath and swing open the door, stepping inside and quickly closing the door behind me. We never cleaned the blood-covered floor, and it has congealed to a thick goo which sticks to my feet as I edge towards the hanging corpse.

"Fucking hell." The rank smell punches me in the guts. I thought I was ready for it, but I struggle to stop myself from gagging while my stomach churns in protest. All the liquid ghastliness inside of me forces its way up my throat and bursts out of my mouth. Trickles of a sickly green colored liquid spew all over the basement floor, mixing in with the dried blood.

Sara's voice squeals behind me. Curiosity got the best of her. I can't stand it in here, not for a second longer, and I run back past Sara, straight to the shower tap in our room, where I fumble to get the water running, then dunk my head in the sink. I gag and convulse violently for a minute straight before the water washes the smell of vomit and the decaying corpse off me.

The water's goddamn cold and sends my body into a shiver. A moment later, I feel Sara shaking me back to reality. I must have zoned out.

"Hank, what the hell are you doing? What, you want to be just like him?" she says angrily, wrapping a towel around me.

"We have to eat," I say weakly.

"So what?" she asks in frustration. "You thought that after all we've endured, you're just going to throw all that away and give in? I know what's behind that door, and I know what he does there. I'm not stupid!"

Like an idiot, I just stare at her while she rambles on. All I can think is, how does she even have the strength to shout right now?

"But if we don't eat soon, we'll die."

"And what's your plan, exactly?" she says. "Chop up that boy into pieces and then feed him to us? No! I'm not letting you do that. Can't you see? This is exactly what he wants!"

"I know, Sara, but we have to eat!"

"He's a person, Hank!" Sara shouts at me. "A human being, just like us! Right now, we have a choice. We can't give in, even if death is the alternative."

I shake my head. "He *was* a person. And Mal won't come back until we've done what he wants us to do. Don't you understand that? He must have a camera here, something to know that we haven't eaten yet!"

"No, Hank!" Sara insists, "he doesn't know. Can't you see? He's trying to mold us into him, so he can justify what he does and not be alone. He doesn't care if we die, because he'll simply replace us with someone new." Sara stops and clenches her stomach, groaning.

"Yeah, but *I* care if *you* die." There's nothing more to say. Keeping Sara alive long enough to escape this place is more important to me than morals. I walk over to my mattress and pick up one of my spare t-shirts. Taking it in both hands, I pull the neck of the shirt apart, ripping it apart. I throw one half back onto the bed. The other, I tie around my face to mask the revolting smell. When I look in Sara's direction, she doesn't say a word in protest. No matter how much she hates the idea, even she knows we won't survive much longer like this. She just needed me to take the lead.

When I walk through the door, the smell smashes me in the guts, but with the cloth wrapped around my face and breathing through my mouth, I know I can survive it. I stare at the hanging body, or at least what remains, and make a sign of the cross on my chest. Poor lad. I figure the first thing to do is just to get rid of the smell as best as I can.

I grab a mop and begin sloshing the thick blood and other bodily liquids that are glued to the floor. Similarly to the basement, there is a gutter built into the floor, into which I guide it all, praying it doesn't get blocked.

I really should have worn something over my shirt. It's damn cold in here, although I can't be complaining. This freezer of a room is the only reason he hasn't gone completely rotten.

After ten minutes of work that takes up most of my depleted energy reserves and has me sweating despite the cold, the majority of the slush is gone. I turn on the tap in the room and let the water spread around the floor, allowing it to wash away the rest of the residue with it. After gallons of water have flooded across it, the floor is no longer sticky, thank God. The smell is ripe, but manageable with my makeshift mask.

I'm not sure even the boy's mother would recognize him now. His skin has turned a pale whitish-blue and when I touch him, he's stone cold but waxy. With a deep breath, I prepare for the grim task ahead, selecting a carving knife, the sharpest one I can find. I don't know where to start, so I decide on the remaining leg, trying to remember what Mal did before. I press the knife into the side of the thigh and slice downwards in a slow and steady fashion, not stopping until I've reached the ankle. By now, much of the blood is a sticky puddle at my feet, although some still trickles out as I pierce the flesh. I stand to the side so that the bulk of it doesn't soak me.

Once I've made the incision, I place the carving knife down on the table and sink my nails into the slits cut into the flesh, then steel myself to do the unthinkable. A shiver runs down my spine as I pull at it. I shake my head and try not to think about the moral aspect of what I'm doing. Tell myself I'm just gutting a fish, or some hunted game. I pull at it again and again until, at last, the skin gives away, peeling off from the flesh with a slow ripping sound. Then, with one continuous jerk, I tear it all off.

With the skin gone, the meat, the veins, and the bone are all laid bare. I feel like I'm back in science class, dissecting an animal. *That's it. I'm just in a science class—no, in medical school—dissecting a dead body in medical school to learn about the human body.* This is not so different, is it? *Except medical students don't eat their cadavers.* I try not to think about this horrific fact.

I roll up the skin and throw it down into the rubbish chute. I won't be needing it anymore. My hands are covered in slime and blood, and whatever other fluids came out of the hiker's corpse. I shudder and somehow hold onto my wits without throwing up this time.

After shaking my hands downward to remove the excess slime, I wash them under the tap by the wall. Won't be needing his foot either, so I grab the saw that Mal had been using and cut it off. The bone there is even tougher than I thought. It takes me a good minute to saw through it. Mal must be stronger than he looks given that he cut through the whole thigh so quickly. No wonder he repelled my attacks.

With the foot severed from the body, I systematically make my way upwards. Within an hour, there is not a shred of skin left on the boy's body. Next, I think back to what Mal told me were the best parts to eat.

Tongue. I reach for it with my hand, but then remember that Mal had already eaten it. I think again. The ribs. I have no idea how I'm gonna do this. I clean away all the human debris and slime from the entrance to his body. Fortunately, Mal has already removed the boy's organs, so my job is easier. I just need to make a bigger incision. When I look around at the wall, a set of large pliers catches my eye. That ought to do it. I walk over and take a hold of them. They are heavier than I expected. I carry them over to the body and position them over one of the boy's ribs and grip them as tightly as I can. Then I take a deep breath and screw my eyes tightly shut.

A loud crack rings out when I press in the plier handles and the rib snaps. There's a sound like a handful of grit hitting tin. Some small fragments of the bone have flown across the room and scattered in different directions at the pressure of the snap. However, I continue with the next set of ribs, then the third, being careful not to pull away any of the meat attached to them. I wouldn't want any of it to go to waste.

Not even halfway through, and I feel drained and want to give up. I don't have the strength for this. Cutting through the flesh is hard work, and cutting through bone is infinitely harder. I can't get used to the smell, either. It's so repulsive I have to step away to a corner and take a breather.

My arms feel like they're about to fall off by the time I'm done with the ribs. I want to admit defeat, but that wouldn't be fair to the boy. He died because of the bloody maniac who wanted to eat him. If anything, the killing would be less justified if we didn't eat as much of him as possible. Perhaps I'm beginning to think like Mal. But I'm only doing this because I want to survive, and to get back at him. Is that enough justification to eat a human being? Maybe I just want to satisfy my insatiable hunger and end the starvation. Or maybe, just maybe, I'm becoming like him. I honestly don't know anymore, and I try not to think about it. My head is too weary to think about it.

Ass. Mal was very enthusiastic when he said the word. I walk around the body and stare at it, trying to figure out the best way to cut it. Without an instruction manual, I just have to wing it and hope for the best. Starting with the left cheek. I carefully cut my way in and work my way around, cutting in a crescent moon shape. My knife is about two inches deep and the meat is so tough that I have to use both hands on the handle.

So close now. With one final slice, the slab of meat falls clean off, plopping onto the bloody floor.

I don't want to spend any longer here than I have to. Exhaustion almost won, and only the prospect of eating keeps me going as I use the last of my feeble strength to saw off all the remaining limbs and the head, then discard them into the rubbish chute. Treating a body like trash gives me a pang of sadness. Nobody should be treated with such disrespect, but the other option was even worse: to let him rot and stink the basement out. *Don't worry, kid, I'll make sure he gets what he deserves.* I don't know if that is true, but it helps to say it to myself.

Once my cleanup operation on the body is done, I grab the mop and start on the floor again. It's not long before the mop head becomes an amalgamation of all the residue that has trickled down from the boy. It's thick and slimy. The metallic smell of blood becomes more pungent as I slush it around the floor. I gag but somehow still keep myself from throwing up. *I'm getting better at this.* The thought is worse than the smell.

When I've finished with the floor, I chuck the ribs and ass-meat in the freezer but keep the thigh out. It's a vast slab of meat, way more than our shrunken bellies will be able to handle, so I cut off just a quarter of it, and stick the rest in the freezer.

I stare at the meat for a few seconds. Dinner for me and Sara.

What have I become?

***

Sara and I look at the two raw slabs of meat for a while, still undecided whether we should eat it. I wait for Sara's judgment. I'll let her make the call.

"We're only doing this to survive," she says. "And we will remember that boy for his sacrifice."

I slap the two slabs of meat in the pan together, adding pepper and salt. Once they're sizzling, the aroma fills the basement, making me forget the stench still lingering from the butchery room. My stomach growls and my mouth salivates. I can see Sara looking at the frying pan with her mouth ajar. I turn the slabs of meat and wait, ignoring my stomach's rumbling calls to rush. It's not worth taking chances with undercooking week-old meat. Once they are blackened on the outside and cooked through, I put them on two plates and push one towards Sara.

After a moment's hesitance, we say a short prayer and grip our knives and forks. Soon, we begin eating in silence, except for the slicing and chewing of cooked meat. The moment I take the first bite, any remaining doubts whether I should eat it disappear. My body thanks me for the meal, for allowing us to survive. It eases the guilt, but we both have tears in our eyes as we consume the hiker boy's flesh.

My appetite partially sated, my thoughts turn back to everything Mal has told me about himself and his reasoning for doing all of this, and I try to dissect it in my head. *This is my communion. In church, we take bread and wine. We commune, we become one with Christ in his body and become one with each other as brother and sister in Christ. In his church, they take it more literally, using blood and flesh.*

It's a challenge, but I try seeing it with Mal's eyes for a moment, and search for his justifications. Being perfectly okay with eating people would suggest that he considers humans as no better than animals, just like cows, chickens, or deer. And we all eat animals, so why should human meat be any different? I remember a scene from a documentary on Planet Earth that I watched. Even other primates, like chimpanzees, resort to cannibalism. In the episode, one family attacks another, killing a young chimp from the opposing family. Rather than letting the meat go to waste, they share and eat the chimp's body. And the documentary reminds the audience that chimpanzees are mostly vegetarian, although they sometimes hunt and kill monkeys. Their own relatives. Well, sort of.

Of course, what he does is abhorrent, but I do kinda understand his church's philosophy on saving mother nature. Humans are the world's apex predators, but we are wiping out animal and plant life faster with every year. Way faster than any other apex predator before us.

"Hank?" Sara's voice calls out and breaks me out of my thoughts.

"Yes?"

"Food's going cold," she says, pointing to my meal. After saying that, she hangs her head, as though she's guilty of a crime.

I put the piece of meat in my mouth and chew, the juices oozing into my overgrowing beard.

"What's on your mind?" she asks me.

"I was just thinking about Mal," I say with a shrug. "Trying to understand him. This church of his has me thinking."

"Still trying to figure out his fucked-up mind?"

I shake my head. "I've already figured him out. He mentioned his church and his beliefs to me the other day, and it got me thinking about his way of life. I guess there is a religious reason behind everything he does."

"Well, their beliefs are quite straightforward. The four pillars."

"Four pillars?" I ask.

"Yeah, the ones he mentioned at dinner before he left. Four strict principles that they all agree on. All that contributes to their goal of saving mother nature."

"Ah, yeah. Like suicide, right?"

"Yeah. The first one is self-sacrifice. Suicide. They are all encouraged to take their lives before they die of natural causes. I'm not sure if he was messing with me, but he told me some crazy stuff about it. I think you were asleep."

"Like what?" I ask her as I lean in closer.

"Well, he was talking about Christmas," Sara says. "It's the day when Jesus was born, right? And we celebrate that day with food and presents."

I nod away, seeing where she's going with this.

"But all this celebrating, it leads to overconsumption of food and too much focus on material gifts, which they view as forms of gluttony and greed, which are actually two sins in Christianity. Pretty much everyone commits these sins, including them, so they settled on a way to counterbalance these sins, to stay in God's good books."

"And what do they do?"

"From what I understood, they offer sacrifices to God every year on Christmas day. I don't know how many or anything, but can you imagine how crazy that sounds?"

"That's pretty extreme," I admit. "But it makes sense in a twisted way. Doesn't it?"

Sara looks at me with a funny look on her face. "Maybe for him."

"Yes, of course," I say, quickly backtracking. "I mean, from his point of view, he's just trying to save the world."

"Religious nut-job, that's what he is," Sara finally says after a long pause.

As we take a few more bites of our steak, the chimp story comes back to my mind. I decide not to ruin her appetite by talking about monkey brain-eating chimps.

"If he really believed in God," Sara says after we've consumed the last morsels, leaving our plates empty, "he wouldn't do this to people. Not to us, not to that guy and all the other poor people he murdered. Nothing he does is going to prevent him from going to hell."

"I agree. If anything, he should catch criminals instead of innocents, people who perhaps even deserve to die."

"Or, you know, don't kill anyone at all and behave like a law-abiding citizen," Sara says with a shrug.

"That works too, I guess." It should be no surprise that Sara disagreed with me on many points. She's young, thinks for herself. Perhaps I'm becoming too agreeable to avoid displeasing either of them.

"You're right about Mal, though," I say.

"What about Mal?"

"That he's a good actor," I say. "The way he lured us both in so easily. And the way he makes even the worst of things sound normal."

"I'm glad that you see through his manipulative behavior," Sara says with a slight smile on her face. "I bet he wants to turn us."

"Turn us?"

"Into fanatical monsters like him," Sara says, not looking at me. "I bet that's what he wants. Other than having some weird, fucked up family, I think he wants to convert us into believers of his faith."

"I can't imagine it's easy getting new recruits when their values are so extreme," I say. "So, what are the other three... three pillars, was it?"

"Yeah," Sara says. "Let me think... so sacrifice. Then, the next one is abortion. To control the human population. Third one is not have sex."

"No sex at all?"

"Just not the normal type," Sara says. "They can suck each other off, you know."

A question enters my mind and I pause as I try to word it properly in my head before voicing it. "Has he... you know?"

Sara gets the gist. "No, he's never laid hands on me," she says. "Not in that way at least. I think he'd rather eat me than fuck me."

I don't know whether to be glad or disgusted.

"And the fourth," Sara says, letting out a deep breath. "Cannibalism." She raises her hands in the air sarcastically and points to our empty plates.

"Mal said something to me that keeps repeating itself in my head." Sara gestures at me to elaborate. "He said he learned early on that if you want something in life, you have to take control and take it for yourself."

"Yeah, well, he wants control, that's for sure," Sara says, her face filled with disgust again.

"Let me guess," I say. "You've seen more, right?"

Sara contemplates, staring into the distance. "Well, yes. I wasn't the first person he dragged down here. There were more before me. I mean, I could tell from all this setup." She gestures around the basement. "I don't know how many there were before me, but there was evidence everywhere. Old clothes, some hair and blood in the corners."

"I can't imagine what it must have been like for you," I say.

"It terrified me. I mean, I haven't even been on a vacation by myself before. Imagine my first trip turning out like this. At first, I thought Mal was just a killer. You know, the typical serial killer like on some tv series. But for some reason, he kept me alive for days and I understood that there was something more to Mal than a sadistic murderer. I had a phase a couple of years ago when I was into psychology, and I think I found a weak point in his mindset. Maybe that's what kept me alive." Sara looks at me. "Or maybe it was blind luck that Mal actually likes me. I really don't know."

"And what happened afterwards?"

Sara thinks for a few moments before answering, "Well, he kept me chained to the wall and fed me meat from the room." She nods at the closed door to Mal's butchery. "About a week after he put me here, he brought down another girl. I think she was older than me, I don't know. She was already drugged, like that hiker guy. Mal was so happy that day. I remember him telling me we'll have fresh meat for dinner that night. I can't believe I never put two and two together."

A chill runs down my spine while I try to push away the vivid picture that springs into my mind.

Sara sees the expression on my face and shakes her head. "Well, it became kinda repetitive afterwards. Mal would bring someone down once every two weeks or so, already drugged. He takes them into that room and comes out alone, extremely happy with himself."

"All girls?" I ask her.

Sara shakes her head. "Not all girls. There were guys as well, but scrawny ones that wouldn't be able to put up a fight. "I guess they're easier for Mal to manage."

"And they were all drugged when he got them here?" I ask. "And you know nothing about them?"

"From what I can tell, all of them were drugged, yes," Sara says. "But I guess he gave them all the same amount of whatever drug he uses, and it affects everyone differently. Some were completely out, while others were barely conscious and tried to open their mouths to talk to me when they saw me in my corner."

I gulp with an awful dawning realization. Some of Mal's victims were awake when he started cutting into them. They probably saw and heard everything happening around them but were unable to act; locked inside their own bodies, perhaps even sensitive to the pain. I close my eyes tightly as a wave of nausea and sympathy threatens to overwhelm me. What suffering Mal has brought upon his innocent victims.

"Now that I think about it, all of Mal's victims were small, like me," Sara says. "Except you, of course. Which means he probably never had the intention of killing and eating you. He really must like you. As a brother."

Lucky me.

16

There's a muffled bang above our heads. Mal's bedroom door. Finally, he's returned. Me and Sara look at each other. I can't quite read the look on her face, somewhere between relief and panic. I really don't want to see the happy sneer on his face when he sees his plan worked out, and I guess she's thinking the same. We sit in silence, ears cupped like eavesdropping kids, with a glass pressed against a wall. As I listen to Mal's footsteps on the floorboards above us, I try to figure out whether there's a second set of footsteps, but it sounds like he's alone.

His steps get closer to the hatch and then halt. As he pulls it open, I count the days he's been away. I think it has been around two weeks, give or take. Ever since eating the hiker, I've been feeling drowsy and drained of all my energy. No matter how much I sleep, it feels like it's never enough. Everything I do is slower, like I've been put under some sort of spell. After the first day of eating, even carving more meat for daily consumption has been a struggle for me. I feel physically weak and drained all the time. Sara told me she was also feeling the same way. There must be something wrong with the meat. I have a feeling it could be the drugs Mal administered into the hiker's body.

He throws down the ladder down the hatch and descends. Sara and I watch in silence. Our reaction time is dulled, and nothing feels real anymore, like a slow-motion replay. The sneer I've been dreading appears on Mal's face when he sees we're alive.

And fuck him. I'm actually quite proud of myself, proud that I've kept me and Sara alive all these days. Despite it going against all the social norms and my principles and all the things I've ever believed in, I'm proud of myself for holding on. I'm proud that even though we're down in this shithole, we're getting by.

Mal has a spring in his step as he moves. His time at the church must have been nice. Looks like he had time to do some shopping, too. He's wearing some new straight-cut jeans, and a belt that I also haven't seen before. It's brown and has a nice brass buckle. Pretty nice shirt on too. It's a sandy brown color, I think, but I am mildly colorblind. Anyway, the shirt's got one of them collars that are pointy. He probably bought it from a vintage store. Nice that he could go shopping for clothes while we were trying to survive down here.

I'm still wearing the used, plain black tee that he got me during my first few days here and a pair of tattered jeans. I turn to Sara. She's already sat cross-legged, back straight, hands on her thighs, hair brushed back behind her ears, and wearing a short dress with flowers on it. It's pretty and colorful, with bursts of red, blue, and yellow.

Mal walks over to Sara and drops two plastic carrier bags on the floor near her.

"How's my baby girl doing?" he asks joyfully.

"I'm fine," Sara says, not putting up as much of an act as she used to.

"How was the trip, Mal?" I ask him, but my head's spinning a little. He has a knife tucked onto the side of his jeans in a leather strap.

All Mal returns is a knowing laugh. "Oh, it was wonderful, Hank," he says. "Quite a drive, but gosh, it was worth it! I spent a few days out there with the church folk. Everyone's excited for Christmas. It's an important occasion for us." He sees me eyeing the bags. "Bought you both some more food. Figured you've grown tired of eating the same thing for the past few weeks."

Without saying a word, I scuttle across to look through the bags. We haven't eaten anything today, so I'm not worried about manners.

"Yeah, dig in guys," Mal says with a laugh. "And then, after eating, how about a board game? You know, the three of us?"

Sara nods as enthusiastically as she can let herself. I take my eyes off the bags and look at her—her eyes are a little droopy. I'm sure mine are, too. Ever since eating the meat, it's like I'm only half *here*, without the energy or strength to fight. I shake my head and turn my attention back towards the bags. Hunger remains a constant issue, and I need to shake this drowsiness off before I think about attacking Mal again.

He's bought lots of stuff. There's canned food—tuna, baked beans, mushrooms, and soup. Underneath that, a few packs of spaghetti, sauces that go along with them, and rice. The second bag is full of bottles of water.

"Happy?" Mal asks, walking over to me and patting me on the shoulder.

"Yeah, thanks," I mutter. My mind is battling itself over and over and over. A part of me wants to turn around, headbutt him, tie him up and leave him here to die. Another part of me tries to feel his emptiness, his honest belief that everything he's doing is for the betterment of the world. I'm completely lost, but Sara keeps her shit together, as usual.

I crack open a tin of tuna and scoop it out with my fingers—the ones I have left, anyway. My mouth salivates as I chew.

"Tuna's tasty, huh?" says Mal, with a knowing grin that I want to smash off his face. "But it doesn't hit the spot like a nice piece of meat, does it?"

Ignoring him, I take another bite, after which my hands are covered in sunflower oil. I bring the can to my mouth and drink the oil inside. Sara follows my lead, taking a can for herself. We both empty our cans in less than a minute, after which my appetite is nowhere near sated, but Mal's set on playing a fucking board game, so Sara rummages through, trying to find something for the three of us to play.

"How about this one?" she asks, holding up Scrabble.

"Sure thing, darling," Mal says. "Let's play that one."

I've never played scrabble and don't care for it. Fact is, I'm not very good with words. Never have been. Even Sally wanted to play one time, but I turned her down.

"Come, sit," Mal instructs as he walks over to the table. He waves me over. He and Sara sit on the floor at the table and start to unpack the board.

"I'm good," I say, holding my palms up. It's no big deal. I just don't want to play.

"This is a family game, Hank," Mal says calmly. "You better come and join us. It won't be much fun with only two of us."

The dangerous tone that accompanies the calmness in his voice conveys a warning, and even in my drowsy and weakened state, I get the message. I sigh, put down my book, and reluctantly join Mal and Sara at the Scrabble board, picking up on a disturbing twinkle in Mal's eyes. Sara's body language is tense. I can't read it like normal. She flashes me a brief, nervous glance—I can't tell if she wants me to play, or bite into Mal's neck again.

The game starts innocuously enough. Mal spells out "family," his voice dripping with a forced joviality that sends a shiver down my spine. Sara follows with "home," as though she wants to trigger him as a punishment in return for leaving us like this.

When my turn comes, I lay down the word "road," forcing a chuckle from Mal.

"Ah, the open road," he says with a sigh. "Hank the trucker. You are missing those long drives, aren't you?"

"It would be nice to get behind the wheel of Midnight again," I say, without looking at him. "I do miss her."

Mal gives me this wicked look as if to say, *your truck's long gone, you'll never see it again.*

The game continues with simple, everyday words. But with each turn, I feel the tension between the three of us rising. It's like we're stepping carefully around fire, each word a step closer to the flames.

Mal places whichever word he can find, with the next one being "turtle." However, Sara takes a subtle jab with "light." It's obvious she could've played a longer word. I stare at my letters. Without thinking much, I spell out "lost."

Mal's demeanor shifts instantly. The air seems to thicken around us. "Lost, huh?" he says, his voice now laced with a cold edge. "You feel lost, Hank?"

I meet his gaze, refusing to back down. "Don't we all, down here?"

Mal's smile disappears. He leans forward, his eyes narrowing. "You think you're clever, Hank?" he asks me, his voice dangerously low. "Are you trying to tell me something?"

I hold his gaze, my heart pounding in my chest. "It's a word, Mal," I say with a shrug. "It's just a game, right?"

Mal stares at me for a long moment, then leans back, forcing a laugh. "Right, just a game," he says, but the friendly facade is gone. "Are you not thankful? If you're unhappy here, do tell."

"We are both thankful, Mal," I say through gritted teeth.

"Feels to me like you've got something to say."

Mal places down five tiles using my "o" from "lost," spelling out "control." I can sense Mal's anger simmering beneath the surface, like a volcano ready to erupt. And I know that one wrong move—one wrong word—could set him off.

Should I go for it? *Screw it.* I want to feel some level of control and to show him I'm not a puppet. Assert some dominance for once, or at least resistance. I lay down my tiles with deliberate slowness. E-S-C-A-P-E. I watch Mal's nostrils flare up as the word forms. He slams his fist onto the Scrabble board, scattering the tiles.

"Escape?" he shouts before his voice becomes a low growl. "You think you can escape me?"

"It's just a word, Mal," I say, refusing to listen to my instincts screaming at me to back down. "It's part of the game. Decent score, too. Twenty points with the double word score."

Mal rises to his feet, his face contorted with rage. "Are you really playing games with me right now, Hank?" he demands. "You think this is all some kind of joke?"

Sara cowers while she tries to plead with him. "Mal, please, we're playing a game. He meant nothing by it!"

But Mal isn't listening. He strides over to me, his hands clenched into fists. "Are you trying to challenge me?" he asks, sounding like a father pushed too far by their offspring. "In my own house?"

I try to keep my voice steady, but my heart is racing and I'm growing dizzier with the loud noises around me. "Mal, calm down," I say. "We're just playing Scrabble."

Mal laughs in my face. "You think you can play me for a fool?" he demands.

Before I can react to that, Mal lunges at me. His hands grab my throat, squeezing tightly. I gasp for air, struggling against his grip. Although I already knew he's strong, his fingers digging into my flesh are like steel traps.

I try to fight back, to push him away, but he doesn't budge. With my drowsiness, my movements are sluggish and uncoordinated. It's like I'm half drunk and half asleep at the same time. Mal puts his face inches from mine.

"You'll never escape me, Hank," he whispers to me. "You belong to me now. You're mine."

I can feel my consciousness giving away and my vision blurring. But then, suddenly, he releases his grip. I collapse to the floor, coughing and gasping for air. Mal stands over me, a smirk on his face.

"You see?" he says, with that horrible sneer on his face. "You're nothing without me. You're weak and helpless."

Sara rushes to my side. "Hank, are you okay?"

I nod, still struggling to catch my breath. "I'm fine," I stutter. "Just... caught off guard. That's all."

Mal watches us with a smug satisfaction before he wags his finger at us and announces, "You're here because I allow it. You live because I allow it. Never forget that. I suspected that you'd plot something whilst I was away, so I made sure that the boy ingested enough sedatives to put a rhinoceros to sleep. All the meat you've been eating has kept you weak."

So, I was right about why both me and Sara have been feeling drowsy. Anger, frustration, and disgust boil inside me like lava, threatening to explode. I should have known he would do something like this to keep us under control.

Mal walks over to us slowly and stops in front of Sara, who is kneeling beside me. He grabs her by the throat and raises her until she's on her feet. I watch him sniff her neck, then her hair, and lick her skin. Her lower lip is quivering, and tears run down her cheeks. But she stays silent, without letting out not so much as a simple whimper. Her self-control amazes me yet again.

"I will never let you go," Mal says into Sara's ear before he pushes her back down to the floor with a thud. "Maybe I've been too kind to you two ungrateful pieces of crap. Despite all the presents I bought you, and my efforts in keeping you well-fed, you throw it back in my face again. The church is right. We become greedy and gluttonous around this time of year. The devil's temptations have gotten to you. We will have to get rid of his hold on you."

17

Mal bolts up the hatch, leaving Sara and me sitting in a stunned silence. As we wait anxiously until he returns, my drowsy mind makes up several scenarios about what Mal might do to us.

I'm confident that death is not on the menu, but further physical harm is a strong possibility. Or perhaps he's decided it's time to discard his playthings and get new ones. Either way, I need to prepare, so I take out the dinner knife from under my mattress and tuck it into my jeans. It's sharp enough now that it might serve as a decent weapon. Now I need these sedatives to wear off so I can meet him on a fair footing.

Sara's humming a nervous tune and biting her fingernails, and there's nothing I can do to comfort her. I have no idea what this psychopath has in store for us. My body grows more tense with every passing minute.

An hour later, the hatch opens and Mal climbs down, holding a bunch of large, thick candles against his chest. He smiles when he sees the confused looks on our faces, but says nothing. The look on his face screams, *I know something you don't.*

He paces around the basement, arranging the candles meticulously in a circle around us—exactly thirteen, by my count. Sara and I look at each other's faces, wary of what is happening.

"Sit," Mal finally commands, and we comply, the circle of candles enclosing us. In the center, Mal draws a symbol and whispers words, quiet enough only for him to hear. I have no idea what the symbol is, but its lines are sharp and jagged.

Mal pauses his muttering and looks up, his gaze piercing mine like he's looking deep into my soul. Then he reaches into a bag he brought down with him and pulls out a small vial. It's dark, with a thick, maroon colored liquid inside.

"This," Mal says, holding the vial up like it's some kind of holy relic, "is the key. It is the path to face your sins, to repent, and to discover yourselves."

What is he's on about? I look over at Sara, who glances back at me like a deer caught in the headlights.

"Drink," Mal orders, thrusting the vial into my hands. I look at it, contemplating, even though I know I have no choice.

"Now!" Mal roars. I bring the vial to my lips, close my eyes, and take a gulp. The liquid is thick and metallic in taste. *Blood!* I gag as it goes down, but it doesn't come back up again. Guess I've gotten used to putting some awful stuff into my stomach, so what's a little more blood?

I pass the vial to Sara, who looks just as afraid as I am. She takes the vial from me and brings it up to her mouth. Her face turns pale as she drinks, but she's stronger than she looks. She doesn't even flinch.

Mal's holding this old, weathered book in his hands. Its pages look like they could crumble to dust any second. He opens it up and begins chanting. It's not in English, though. The chanting is in an older language that's harsh and guttural. Perhaps Latin.

As he recites, I feel the hairs on the back of my neck stand up. The long shadows cast by the flickering flames make Mal's face seem even more contorted.

I look at the book he's holding up with my eyes narrowed and catch the name on the cover. *The Satanic Bible.*

I try to focus on the sound of Mal's voice, but it becomes increasingly difficult as a strange sensation creeps over me. I start to hear things—whispers, almost inaudible, coming from the shadows in the room. Sara seems to notice them too, her gaze darting around the basement, searching for the source.

Now and then, Mal stops reading and looks at us, his gaze intense and piercing. It's like he's expecting something to happen. Almost as if he is waiting for a sign. He then dives back into his book, the words pouring out of him faster and faster in a chant that seems to last forever.

The basement grows colder and the air heavier. I don't think we're alone anymore. I try to shake the feeling off, telling myself it's only our old friend fear playing tricks on my mind.

But then I see it—or rather, feel it. A presence, something lurking just beyond the edge of the candlelight. It's like nothing I've ever experienced before. A chill runs down my spine, and for a moment, I swear I see a shadow move, independent of the flickering flames.

Mal doesn't seem to notice, though. He's lost in his own world, consumed by whatever ritual he's performing. The chanting reaches a crescendo and as it does, my head spins. The room tilts as if I'm strapped into a carnival ride, and the candles blur into streaks of light. Everything goes black. I'm falling, or maybe floating, into a darkness that's as absolute as it is terrifying.

The last thing I remember is Mal's voice, still chanting, as I succumb to the void.

18

I float aimlessly, disconnected from my body. All the sounds I hear are muffled, like I'm submerged underwater, but I can sense the ritual continuing as Mal's voice continues to echo and drone from a million miles away.

I try to open my eyes, to break free from this trance, but my eyelids are unresponsive, like they've been weighted down, or stapled shut. Panic sets in. Am I dying? Is this what it feels like to have your soul ripped away?

Then, amidst the darkness, I see shapes forming. Vague outlines at first, like shadows dancing on the periphery of my vision. They grow clearer, more distinct. Figures, human-like but distorted, as if made of smoke and mist. They circle around us, their movements synchronized with Mal's chants.

The basement fades away, replaced with a church. An old one, with thirteen large columns running down on each side. Beside each column, a different holy figure is depicted, carved from the same stone as the column itself. And above them hangs the same sort of symbol that Mal drew on the floor in front of us. It is some sort of star.

I find myself sitting on one of many church benches. There's at least a dozen on either side of the center aisle. In front of me lies the altar, from which a shadowy shape forms into a person and steps towards me.

Sally. She takes small steps towards me, wearing a wedding dress, only it's not white, but black. She stops just two meters from me. Not a single muscle in her face appears to move, as though she is frozen in time. Then she speaks.

"I've missed you, my love."

"Sally," I can't tell if I am saying her name aloud, or in my head. To me, it is all the same. "I miss you, too. So, so much."

"Don't be sad. When it is your time, we will lie in our beautiful garden together. But first, you must save the girl and repent. Only then will your sins be forgiven."

I stand and step out to the aisle, taking hold of both her hands in mine. "I've missed you so much, Sally," I mutter, overwhelmed with emotion. "I can't believe you're here." A solitary tear escapes. My heart races.

Sally pulls one of her hands away and points at my chest.

"What are you doing?" I ask her, confused.

Her finger strikes my chest, and sends me flying backwards through the benches, through the church wall and out into a blank white floating space. I look around. There's nothing else but a sea of white. Before I can say or do anything, gravity kicks in and I fall. I keep falling and falling, my body twisting and turning like a ragdoll. Then, with a loud thud, I hit the floor of the church again. Looking up, Sally is standing above me, with the same deadpan look in her eyes.

"You can save yourself," she says. "But you must repent your sins. Before it's too late."

I try to speak but I can't. Suddenly, the surrounding air grows colder. Another voice joins in with Sally's, chanting in unison, "Repent. Repent for your sins. The birth of the son of God is nearly upon us."

I hear a guttural croaking from behind, and I turn my head and nearly jump out of my skin, bashing an elbow against the bench in front of me. My eyes widen. Sitting there is a giant toad five times my size.

"This toad represents greed," Sally says. "It wanted to live both on land and water, unable to just choose one part of the universe like all the other animals. This toad has grown so massive because it embodies your own greed."

"Sally, my love, please," I try to plead with her, my heart racing. "Stop this. It's not like you."

I'm in an internal battle, with half of me desperately wanting to believe that the Sally standing in front of me is real, and the other half objectively knowing her not to be.

I try to step towards her again, to break her out of her trance. Before I can make more than one step, the toad leaps up into the air, shaking the ground. As it jumps higher and higher, the roof of the church rises with it.

I dive out of the way. Hallucination or not, I'm not risking getting crushed by a mammoth toad. My body collides with the hard church floor and the pain seems real enough. A thick cloud of dust settles around me, irritating my lungs, causing me to break into a coughing fit.

"Don't be greedy, for a greedy person is an idolater, worshiping the things of this world, Colossians 3:5," Sally's voice calls through the dust.

I stare at her while she rambles on. Her eyes are like ice, her voice a chilly wind cutting through me. What happened to the warm, loving wife I remember so fondly?

"Greed," she says. "Taking more than you give, caring only for your own desires. Think of the little things. The trash you'd toss without a second thought, rather than giving to charity. The gas you guzzle driving that big old truck."

"Sure, I ain't no saint, but I have done nothing others don't," I say in protest. But it's pointless. A huge weight presses on me, like I'm carrying every piece of trash, every excess, every hurt I've caused.

"You see, Hank?" Sally's voice is now a whisper, a blade slicing through my defenses. "Your greed. It's taken more than you know."

I stand up from the floor and bolt for the church doors, the heavy steps of the monstrous toad thundering behind me. My heart's pounding in my ears, each thud a deafening echo in the cavernous space. The air feels thick, almost suffocating as I push through it like an infant emerging from the womb, desperation fueling my every move as the light grows closer.

I reach the doors and push them open with a force I didn't know I had left in me. The toad's croaks are right on my heels, a wet, guttural sound that sends shivers down my spine. I don't dare look back.

Instead, I slam the church doors shut behind me, the sound echoing through the now eerily quiet space. My breaths come in ragged gasps, my hands shaking as I lean against the cold, hard wood of the door.

A moment of silence descends before a soft thud echoes through the door. My heart skips a beat, but the door holds, and the thing on the other side leaves. I slide down to the floor, trying to catch my breath, trying to make sense of what just happened.

As my breathing steadies, I look around. I'm no longer in the church. Instead, I find myself transported to a new setting. It's a banquet hall, but not like any I've ever seen. The tables are laden with food, mountains of it, overflowing plates and platters. The smell is intoxicating, a mix of roasted meats, fresh bread, sweet pastries—all the things I've loved and indulged in without a second thought. But there's something off about it. The food looks too perfect, too abundant. It's like a scene out of a fairytale—or a nightmare.

As I stand, the table's centerpiece draws my attention. It's a pig, but it's unlike any pig I've ever seen—massive, bloated, its skin a sickly pale color. Suddenly, it's no longer in the middle but sitting at the head of the table, like some grotesque parody of a king. The pig's eyes meet mine and there's an intelligence present that shouldn't exist, as if it knows me, knows my deepest, darkest thoughts and desires.

"This is the embodiment of over-eating, Hank," Sally's voice whispers in my head. "This bloated pig."

A wave of nausea hits me as I look at the creature, its snout twitching as if it can smell my fear, my guilt.

"You've indulged too much, Hank," Sally's ethereal, floating voice continues. "You've taken more than your share, more than you need. This is your sin, the sin of gluttony."

I try to turn away, to escape the accusing gaze of the pig, but my feet are rooted to the spot. The banquet hall spins, the feast blurring into a whirl of colors and smells.

"You must face it, Hank," Sally's voice insists in my head. "You must face your sin, then confront it."

I close my eyes, trying to shut out the overwhelming sights and sounds, but it's no use. The smell of the food, the pig's vile presence, it's all-consuming.

When I open my eyes again, the pig is closer, its breath a mix of decay and sweetness. I feel its hot breath on my face, and I know I can't run from this, from what I've done, from who I've become.

"You must repent, Hank," I hear Sally's voice in my head again, a finality in its tone that leaves no room for argument.

The pig watches me, its eyes unblinking as I stand there, facing my darkest self.

The roof of the banquet hall suddenly shatters, raining down shards of wood and plaster. A deafening croak thunders through the air as the colossal toad crashes down from above, landing in front of me with a ground-shaking thud. My heart races as I witness these two grotesque giants—the toad and the pig—standing face-to-face with me.

The toad, its skin a sickly green, oozing a mucus that glistens in the dim light, its eyes bulging and unblinking. The way it moves, each hop sending tremors through the floor.

The pig, its massive, bloated body heaving with each breath. Its skin, unnaturally pale and stretched tight over its engorged form, with eyes small and beady, fixed on me and burning with stark intelligence. Its snout twitches and I can almost hear it sniffing the air, drinking in my delicious fear.

The two beasts circle me. Their movements are slow and deliberate, tormenting me as if they know there's no escape. The toad's croaking and the pig's grunting fill the air, making my skin crawl.

I feel trapped, caught between these two symbols of my greed and gluttony. Tears form in my eyes as the reality of what I'm facing hits me. I've sinned, hurt people, taken more than my share. I've lived a life of excess, never thinking of the consequences, never considering the pain I might be causing others.

Weeping openly now, I fall to my knees and beg forgiveness. "I'm sorry," I sob through my tears. "I'm so sorry, Sally. I've been greedy and selfish. I never meant to hurt anyone, and I especially never meant to hurt you."

One-by-one, I'm forced to face all my sins, every single one, in a relentless montage. I confess everything, pouring out my guilt and regret. The time when I was working as a gas station pump attendant, and we were supposed to share our tips, but I kept twenty dollars all for myself. The time I sneaked into the pantry and guzzled slices of birthday cake before it was even my birthday, then tried to make it look whole again.

And then, in her own sweet voice, gentle and loving, I hear Sally say, "It's not your time yet, Hank."

"I miss you, Sally," I whisper, my voice choked with emotion. "I miss you so much."

Then, as quickly as it appeared, the light fades, and I'm plunged back into darkness. But this time, it's different. The oppressive feeling is gone, the air no longer heavy with malice. I look up through my tears and the beasts have vanished. The banquet hall, the shattered roof, all of it has disappeared. I'm back in the basement with the circle of candles around me.

I take a deep, ragged breath, trying to ground myself back in this grim reality. My gaze shifts between Sara and Mal. Sara's still lost in her own hallucinations, her body twitching sporadically. I can only imagine the horrors she's facing in her mind, the sins she's being forced to confront. The sight of her struggle wrenches my heart.

Mal, however, watches us with a calm, almost satisfied look. His eyes, fixed on Sara, seem to relish every twitch and enjoy every faint murmur that escapes her lips. It's sickening to watch this man playing God with our minds. It's clear he knows exactly what kind of torment we're experiencing, and he's been through it himself. What awful visions did he witness?

I rub my eyes, trying to shake off the lingering effects of the hallucinogens. But even as the more vivid images fade, whispers and shadows linger at the edge of my perception. I hear faint voices, unintelligible but insistent, as if they're trying to tell me something important. Shadows flicker and dance in the corners of my eyes. I no longer know what's real and what's not. Logically, it must be the aftereffects, remnants of the drug coursing through my veins. But in the dim, flickering candlelight of the basement, every shadow hides a lurking presence, and every whisper carries a secret message meant only for me.

I glance at Sara again, her face still contorted in distress. I want to reach out, to offer her some sort of comfort, but I'm frozen, trapped in my seat by the chains of my uncertainty. The memory of Sally's words haunts me, along with the surreal confrontation with my sins. It's like I'm caught between two worlds, unable to fully return to either.

Mal breaks the eerie silence, his voice slicing through the basement. "It's a cleansing process," he says, almost thoughtfully. "Confronting our inner demons, our darkest fears. It's how we grow, how we become better."

I want to scoff, to yell at him for his madness, but my throat has tightened, making my voice a mere croak. Instead, I just watch, a silent observer to this macabre ritual. I can't help but wonder what Mal saw in his own visions, what twisted justifications his mind conjured to excuse his actions. Or perhaps this ritual is to cleanse the sins, and he never needed to justify or excuse, only accept them.

As the whispers continue to murmur in my ears, I try to stay alert. I want to focus on Mal, to watch him for any sign of vulnerability or weakness. I need to be ready for myself and for Sara. Whatever Mal's plans are, I can't let him win. I have to find a way to fight back and escape this nightmare. But for now, all I can do is wait, watch, and listen to the whispers of my own haunted mind.

Sara suddenly jerks upright, her eyes snapping open, drenched in sweat. She gasps for air, flailing around wildly, as if waking from a nightmare. Her eyes spin around the room until her shocked gaze locks onto mine, confusion clouding her eyes. Slowly, her tense body relaxes as she readjusts to normality. Were her visions as wild as mine?

The three of us sit in uneasy silence, the only sound being our ragged breaths and the soft flickering of the candles. I watch Sara, her chest heaving, trying to make sense of what just happened. Her eyes meet mine again, this time filled with a silent plea for understanding, as though I've seen her deepest, darkest deeds.

Mal breaks the silence in his usual, calm voice. "You've both been through a journey. A most necessary journey that will change your life for the better," he announces. "The spirits have shown you what you needed to see. It's a part of our ritual, our way of cleansing the soul."

I stare at him, my chest a tangle of anger, confusion, and an unexpected sense of relief. Yes, relief. I hardly believe it. I don't know whether it is because the hallucinations are over or whether it is because of the hallucinations I saw, but I have a new sense of inner peace. Perhaps it is acceptance.

Amid this insanity, confronting those visions, those sins, is like a release to me. I feel liberated, in a way. I can't describe it in words. It feels like shedding a weight I'd been carrying without knowing. It was excruciating and terrifying, of course, but in some twisted way, it is also freeing. Yes, the more I think about it, the stronger the feeling grows, until I feel more at peace with myself than

I was when I was driving Midnight all alone through long roads.

"You've faced your demons," Mal says, breaking the silence. It's almost as if he was party to my private thoughts. "You've repented. That's the first step towards salvation, towards being part of our family. From the moment I met you both, I sensed the darkness you both hid. Not just from the world, but from yourselves. By confronting them, you have confronted your past deeds, some of which you may have been embarrassed about, maybe even feared."

I don't respond. Part of me wants to suffocate him, to end his goddamn games. I'm not a lab rat he can just experiment with, nor am I part of his twisted idea that we're a family. But a strange part of me actually feels thankful towards him because what he says is exactly how I feel. But I'm determined not to submit to his ideas. Even though my heart feels at ease because I really do feel like I've faced my demons, my head encourages me to keep fighting back against Mal and not to submit to his control. And after today, I'm certain that Mal is not an ordinary psychopath who just kills people for sadistic pleasure. He is much more than that. He is deeply religious in a weird, twisted way, and it gives him a godly sense of control and power over what he does without guilt. But then I suppose all serial killers are like that. Call it extreme egotism, but all of them must find an excuse to do what they do and be what they are.

I stare at Mal, wanting to hate him. Even though I feel unburdened, I should still despise Mal for putting me and a poor, innocent girl through this. I want him to suffer in the worst way possible. I grit my teeth and try to clench my fists, but my energy levels are not back to normal yet. My fingers feel numb, and I can't even flex my muscles. The blood Sara and I drank must have been laced with some kind of strong hallucinogenic to send us through all those vivid visions. Faint echoes and whispers still trail all around me. I try to shake my head to clear them, but my body screams in protest. I suppose a week of eating that sedated meat has also gotten us pretty good. All these substances swirling around my system. Who knows what they've done to me? Anger bubbles up inside me. I must keep reminding myself Mal is far more intelligent and strategic than I give him credit for.

19

Mal takes his time to brush off the shape he drew on the floor before he removes the circle of candles. I'm halfway back to reality, but a part of me still watches out for those giant creatures, still hearing faint noises I know aren't real.

Sara's her eyes are puffy, and her hands are shaking. I want to ask her what *she* saw, but her expression says she wants to be left alone.

Once Mal's finished cleaning up, he straightens himself to look at both Sara and me, appraising the state we're in. The satisfactory look he had on his face earlier is now gone, but he doesn't look concerned, either.

"I have to confess something," Mal says once he's taken all the candles away.

"What is it?" Sara asks.

"I suppose I over-salted the meat, didn't I?" Mal chuckles.

Sara furrows her arched eyebrows. "What do you mean?"

"Oh, just the sedatives I forced down that boy's mouth, I mean," Mal says, as if it is the most casual thing in the world. "Maybe I overdid it. We should probably just chuck out the remaining meat."

"Why did you fill him with sedatives?" I ask, knowing the answer already.

"Well, for starters, I didn't want to come back and get stabbed with kitchen utensils, or worse, butchered with my own tools, Hank. Do understand, I like you. I really do. But I know you're a feisty one. So, this was just, you know, a sort of safe way for me to leave you two alone in here. But from now on, I'm gonna change my methods. I'll just administer you both with a daily dose of a mild sedative," Mal says, as if he's nothing more than a friendly doctor dispensing innocent medicine.

When he laughs, I feel a chill in my bones. "For everyone's safety. I mean, look at us," he says, pointing to his neck and to me. "It's not sustainable, living like we have. You're out here looking like Frankenstein's monster—missing fingers, fingernails, bite marks all over you, bruises on your face. Even poor Sara got a nasty bump on her head."

The way he says it makes it sound like it's all my fault, yet I can't come up with a counterargument. Do I blame myself for all the consequences Sara and I have endured? After all, I instigated them all. Mal's played me again.

"Now," Mal says, rubbing his palms together, and smiles to himself. "Why don't you help me clean up, Hank? I'm sure it will get your mind off things."

I shrug. It's not like I can protest, anyway—no energy for it. I help Mal put the food away and clean up the basement.

Once that is done, Mal walks into his butchery while I collapse on my mattress, rubbing my eyes, as if that's going to wipe the hallucinogenic drugs out of my system. I can feel Sara's eyes burning into me. I rest my spinning head against my hands, hoping for relief, but it doesn't help. The butchery door opens and Mal steps back into the room.

"Thanks for cleaning up in there, guys. Or was it just you, Hank? Something tells me Sara didn't get involved. There was no point keeping that boy around when he's been left out for so long. Anyway, I'm going out hunting. Keep your fingers crossed. Hopefully I'll be back with something nice and fresh tonight!"

Knowing that yet another innocent soul is going to fall prey to this monster, and I can do nothing to stop it, makes my heart ache.

Mal grabs a clear glass vial and injects a syringe in it, similar to how he did when he was sedating me to prepare for my head stitches. "You two will be fine. Don't you worry about it," he assures us. "It's just something to relax you a little."

He ushers Sara to him, and she looks at him with alarm in her eyes.

"Don't worry, baby," Mal coos. "It won't do anything to you. It will help you relax. I promise. Would Daddy ever hurt you like that?"

When she doesn't move, he signals her forward with an impatient gesture. Sara hauls herself up and Mal welcomes her into his arms gently and strokes her hair, muttering something inaudible. I can't watch and I look away in disgust. Then I hear Sara gasp and look up to see that Mal has stuck the syringe into her arm. He pulls it out slowly and guides her towards her corner. In a daze, she weaves back to where she was sitting previously and slumps down.

Then Mal refills the syringe and looks at me. I know I have no choice but to go over to him. I do so without him having to ask me.

"That's a good boy, Hank. Now, hold steady."

He jabs the needle into my arm. I don't feel anything, to be honest. Maybe it is because of the hallucinogens, I don't know. Once he takes the needle out, I have no choice but to walk back and collapse to the floor, just like Sara did.

"Okay!" Mal says happily. "Now, you two be on your best behavior until I come back with fresh meat, okay?" He picks up the candles and climbs up the ladder, disappearing through the hatch. The hatch door shuts with a creak and it's just Sara and me alone in the basement once again. My head fogs up inside. The walls seem to be getting closer and closer together, and the air's thickening.

No matter how I sit, my mattress feels like a rock. Sara's gone totally quiet, all curled up on her own, looking like she's a million miles away. I try to say something, break the silence, but my words come out all wrong, slurred. The sedative is doing its job. "Sara," I manage to get out of my mouth, but it's barely legible.

"I'm beginning to lose hope," she says, considering each word, each letter even, like it's an enormous effort to speak. "I don't feel anything anymore. What's the point of living like this?"

"You can't think like that. I made you a promise, and I intend to keep it."

She smiles dreamily. "You've tried, Hank, you have. You've given it your all. I can't thank you enough for it. But it's time to face reality."

"When Mal gave us the blood... that hallucinogen, or whatever that vial contained, I saw my wife. She opened my mind to everything wrong I have done in my life, things to be ashamed of. But I also saw all the good I can do with the time I have left in this world. Sally may not be here, nor Olivia, but I have you. I made a promise to keep fighting for you, for as long as I breathe."

A tear escapes Sara's eye as she crawls over to hug me. My eyes well up, and before I know it, we're both bawling our eyes out, our bodies entwined as one.

***

"I was just thinking of the two other girls who were here before you arrived," Sara says. "Amy and Lily were their names."

Were their names. Past tense. No questions need to be asked about what happened to them. Not here.

"Amy was already here when Mal threw me in."

"What happened?" I ask, sitting with my back against the wall, listening.

"She was on the floor, already bloody with cuts all over," Sara says, her eyes expressive, as though reliving that day. "When I saw her, I knew that begging for my life would be hopeless, so when he strapped me to the chair, I just gave in. I didn't see any point in fighting fate. I didn't make a sound when he cut the piece from my thigh. I didn't want to give him the satisfaction. But he didn't seem to like that." She shakes her head as though the moment is happening all over again, her voice growing more animated. "He was angry that I wasn't fighting death. It's as though he justifies killing people because they're attached to life. But when he saw I wasn't going to fight it, he put down his scalpel."

"What happened then?"

"He disappeared back up the ladder for a few hours. At that point, the anxiety had built up inside me to the point I had a full-on panic attack. Took a while to calm myself down. When I came to my senses, I realized that the girl on the floor, Amy, was asking for help in this tiny, weak voice, over and over again. It's like she was stuck in a loop. I think she'd lost a lot of blood, so it was hard for me to get any sense out of her."

There's a slight coolness in Sara's recollection of events, as if she's distanced herself from what happened all these weeks ago. "You must have been scared out of your mind."

"I was," Sara says, chewing her lip. "As soon as Mal came back, he dragged her off into the butchery by her hair. She screamed her lungs out, begging for mercy, and all I could do was watch. When Mal shut the door behind them, the screaming ended in an instant. But I could still hear her broken voice echoing through the walls for days after that. Mal started frying up steaks that same evening. I hadn't the slightest clue that it was *her*."

"So, Mal gets off on us trying to escape, but begging has the opposite effect."

Sara nods. "And the other girl, Lily. She lasted longer. Mal brought her in a week later. He beat her pretty badly because she kept screaming. He said she gave him a headache. But even then, she kept relentlessly kicking at the wall with the heel of her boot. I admired her effort for the first hour, maybe two, but then even I got a headache and told her to shut up. I didn't expect myself to lash out like that. Maybe acting tough in front of her was my way of masking my fear."

"It's not your fault, Sara. Being trapped in a place like this messes with your head."

"Anyway, she learned quickly what kind of man Mal was," she says. "I convinced her to stay silent and to do as he said. But she only lasted a day. When Mal tried brushing her hair, she went crazy. Wouldn't stop making a racket even when he went back upstairs."

"And he snapped?"

Sara nods. "Mal dragged her into that room by her hair," she says. "It gave me all these flashbacks to when I was younger. My dad getting drunk, taking out his stress on me and momma."

We lock eyes for a few moments. Then I stand up from my mattress, walk across the room, and slump down next to her, putting my arms around her.

"You don't deserve any of what has happened to you, Sara. Remember that." I lift her chin up. "You're stronger than you think."

She leans into my chest and snuggles closer, so I can feel her heart beating faster and faster against mine. I rub her back with one hand while the other hand pulls her in tighter towards my chest. I want her to feel safe, and I want her to know that I'm here for her, but my body is on autopilot, reacting to my senses. My hand caresses Sara's long, blonde hair. A nostalgic feeling hits me—holding Sally in my arms after a long day of work. Sara leans back and looks up at me.

I lower my head and close my eyes until my lips collide with hers.

My body seizes control from my rational mind. My last thought is *how far am I prepared to push the boundaries*? I lean in and give her a small peck on the back of her neck, expecting her to pull away from me, but she grabs me even tighter, digging her nails into my back. I respond, kissing her neck some more, grabbing her hair with one hand and her waist with the other.

She lets out a moan, and I hold her tighter as instinct drives me forward. As her back arches, she looks into my eyes. She holds eye contact for a few seconds, then studies my lips. I take it as a cue, bringing my lips to hers. The first kiss is innocent enough, gentle. A craze washes over me, making me go in for a second. It's almost impossible to resist, but just as my lips are about to reach hers, I stop myself. My brain whirs back into gear moments before there's no going back.

"We shouldn't," I whisper, my forehead resting against hers.

"I know," Sara says softly.

I wonder what she's thinking. A sudden dam bursts inside me and I can no longer contain my urges. It's just me and her in this damp basement, locked away for an eternity. I'll probably never see the world beyond this cracked ceiling again.

I lose myself once again, going back in for a passionate kiss. Her lips are soft, warm, heavenly. Her hands grasp my hair and pull my face even further towards hers.

I gently slide my hands down her shoulders, then to her chest. They're perfect breasts. Perky. She follows my lead as I slide my tongue into her mouth. A euphoric rush hits me. Sara moans, grasping me all over. Her hand brushes over my junk, then starts exploring more eagerly. I cup her breasts, unable to get enough of them. Slowly, I slide one of my hands down to her pussy. So warm. I want to be inside. I lift my head, looking her in the eyes. The seductive look she gives back is all I need to know. I pick her up by her thighs and gently lay her down onto my mattress.

As I kiss her body, I make my way down. Sara undoes the button on her skirt. I offer a hand, unzipping it and pulling it off. I chuck it to the side and look down at her plain white panties. As I reach down to remove them, she grabs my arm, stopping me.

"Be gentle, please," she whispers. "Take it slow."

"Of course," I say, leaning down to kiss her on her inner thighs. Her back arches. With every kiss, I move my way up, gently caressing her soft body along the way. With every one of her moans, I feel myself getting harder.

When I reach her panties, I gently pull them down.

"Hank," she whispers.

"Yeah?"

"It's my first time," she says.

Her words catch me off guard. I lift my head and look at her. Whatever look I have on my face must have made her uncomfortable, because she pulls away, covering herself with the paper-thin duvet.

"Sorry, didn't mean to..." she says awkwardly.

"No, you did nothing wrong. I shouldn't have reacted like that."

"I don't want to die a virgin," Sara admits, her head low, eyes looking down at the mattress.

Die? I want to shout out that she's crazy for thinking that. You're not dying here, don't be ridiculous. But I can't be sure. And dying a virgin? That really would be tragic. Can I allow that to happen?

"Don't feel embarrassed," I whisper. "Really."

"I'm already eighteen, Hank," Sara says, now looking at me. "Of course I'm embarrassed." She sits up, hugging the duvet against her chest. "It feels so embarrassing being in conversations with my friends, when they talk about their amazing sex with their boyfriends and me having to pretend like I know what it's like."

"If it makes you feel any better, I didn't lose my virginity until I was eighteen too," I say to her with a smile. "You shouldn't feel even a tiny bit ashamed."

"Thanks, Hank," she says, her face lightening up a bit.

"We don't have to do it if you don't want to," I tell her. I'm not a monster like Mal, even if my insides are screaming for her.

"No. I want to. You make me feel comfortable," Sara says, looking directly at me. "Hank, I want my first time to be with you."

20

I awake with two sets of footsteps walking on the floor above us. Sara's awake too. We give each other a knowing look and sit up, then scooch with our backs against the wall.

The hatch door opens, and the ladder lowers. Mal clambers down, with a woman thrown over his shoulder like a ragdoll. Once he reaches the basement floor, he drops her half-conscious body to the ground. She's skinny, with disheveled hair and smeared makeup.

"Did I wake you?" He asks.

"Yeah," I grunt.

"Sorry about that. This is Tina," Mal announces with a twisted grin, as if presenting a prize. "I met her at a bar this evening. She needed a lift and, well, I offered to take her home. I'm sure you can guess the rest!"

She sure picked the wrong guy to ask for a ride. Tina slurs something incoherent, her words lost in a drug-induced stupor.

"She looks and smells fresh, don't you think?" Mal asks us, taking a long sniff of her hair, his nostrils flaring with satisfaction. It sends an involuntary shiver down my spine. Then Mal maneuvers Tina to the seat in the far corner of the basement and straps her in, tightening the straps around her arms and then her legs. Her head periodically flops forward. Each time, Mal forcefully pushes it back against the headrest.

"Hank," Sara whispers. "We have to do something."

My promises to her reel through my head.

Mal steps back, admiring his handiwork. "Perfect," he mutters to himself. Then, turning to us, he says, "Tina here is going to be staying with us for just a short while!"

After Mal administers our sedatives—only a mild dose this time, he tells us—I force myself to speak before I get too drowsy to articulate. "Why did you bring her here, Mal?"

Mal chuckles, as if I've asked an amusing question. "Come on, you know why. We can't just starve to death. We've got to eat. Plus, I want to practice what I've been taught at the church."

"Practice what?" I ask, but Mal doesn't reply. "She's drunk, Mal. She doesn't even know where she is."

"That's the beauty of it, Hank," Mal says at last. "She won't remember a thing. A blank slate, if you will."

The casualness in his voice sickens me. Sara grabs a tight hold of my hand, sending my thoughts spiraling through all the things Mal might do to Tina in front of our eyes.

Mal circles the girl, like a predator sizing up its prey. "Fresh, healthy, full of life," he observes. "She's perfect."

I can't hold back anymore. "Perfect for what, Mal? Whatever you're planning to do to her, I beg you to stop."

Mal stops and turns to face me. "Oh, Hank, always so concerned," he says, shaking his head at me, his errant little schoolboy who won't learn.

Sara finally finds her voice. "You can't do this, Mal," she says. "Let her go, please. We're not that hungry."

Mal's expression darkens. "And what would you have me do, Sara?" he demands in a rough voice. Sarcasm drips from his words. "Release her? Let her tell the world about our happy little family? You'd love that, would you?"

"You're sick, Mal," I say, my voice filled with disgust. I also want to turn his attention away from Sara. I don't want her getting hurt. "This isn't right. You can't just kidnap people, drug them, and—"

"I can do whatever I please, Hank," he hisses, stepping closer and towering over me. "This is my world. You're just living in it."

Mal returns his attention to the helpless drunk girl, slumped in the chair. His hand reaches out towards her, tenderly brushing her hair back from her face. "I'll take care of her, don't you worry," he says, almost to himself. "She'll be just fine with Uncle Mal."

Sara's hands clench into fists. "Mal, think about what you're doing!" she pleads.

But Uncle Mal's not listening. Seems like he's already decided. After observing his prize, he disappears through the purple door to his butchery. Minutes stretch like hours until I hear wheels against the concrete floor and, at last, Mal emerges, pushing the metal trolley. It clinks with an assortment of medical and surgical tools.

"I'll be conducting a few experiments on Tina. Although I appreciate the complexities of the human body, I still have much to learn. You're more than welcome to watch, Hank." He turns to Sara. "As for you, young lady, I think you're actually too young to be seeing this, so just read one of your books or something."

Mal picks up a scalpel from the trolley, examining its sharp edge with a studious fascination. "The human body is a remarkable thing, so resilient, yet so fragile," he announces, looking like some kind of twisted professor. Then he turns to Tina, scalpel poised. "Don't worry, Tina. You won't feel a thing."

Sara grips my hand tightly, her nails digging into my skin, her body trembling beside me. I want to shout and scream, to stop Mal in his tracks somehow, but we're powerless, mere spectators in his twisted theater.

I watch as Mal rips open her blouse, and clinically slices into the skin of her chest. His silver scalpel is quickly painted red. Tina's eyes shoot open and she lets out a piercing scream, making both me and Sara jump.

"Help, help me!" She shouts and screams on a loop, pulling at the restraints, her face filled with horror.

"Fuck," is all Mal can manage. "Hank, quickly, I need your help." He unclasps his set of keys and throws them to me.

Sara looks at me in shock. Mal must be completely delusional. I use one of the keys to undo my shackle, then discreetly push the keys over to Sara. As I stand, a vicious head rush hits me, nearly toppling me back down.

"Quick," Mal urges, shouting over Tina's awful screams. "Grab me a sock or something."

I do as he asks, taking a stinking gray cotton sock off my foot and handing it to him. Mal scrunches it up and shoves it into the girl's mouth.

"Shut the fuck up!" he shouts, backhanding her across the face.

"What exactly are you trying to do?" I ask.

"I want to see her beating heart." Mal says it as though it's the most normal thing in the world, like a kid demanding the latest toy. He gestures to her chest. "Hold down on the opening here, whilst I get the numbing agent."

"Mal, I'm not going to let you kill her." It's a dumb thing to say. I don't know why I did. Antagonizing him will not help me save Sara, especially whilst we're both drugged up. I place my palms on the girl's chest, feeling her rapid heartbeat.

"I wasn't planning on killing her. Well, not yet, at least. Just wanted to have some fun. No need to get all fiery." Mal laughs it off. "If you really want, we'll do it the *proper* way," he says, gesturing with air quotes.

"The proper way?" I ask. Mal ignores me, sifting through various vials in the trolley. Tina tries to say something, but her words are muffled. All I understand are her tears.

"I really wanted this to be fun," Mal says with a hint of sadness, "but I guess you'll learn a lot more this way."

He picks up two syringes and injects her twice. "Two separate drugs. Fentanyl and Propofol. Used for general anesthesia. She won't feel a thing," he says confidently.

"How do you know all this?"

"Research, obviously." Mal turns away, reading the labels on his other vials. "Haven't you ever wondered what a beating heart would look like? Not like in some stupid movie scene, but the real thing."

I grab onto the side of the chair to keep myself from stumbling over. His *mild* sedative is really playing a number on me. "No, not really."

"Rocuronium, just what we need," says Mal, jabbing a syringe into the vial.

"And what does that do, exactly?" I ask, my words slurring.

"A paralytic. A muscle relaxant of sorts. To make sure she doesn't move during the procedure."

"Are you sure she won't be in pain?"

"What are you, her friend? Why do you even care?"

"She's a living person," I say slowly, as if explaining to a child. "Can't you feel empathy towards someone in pain? If you're going to do these awful things, at least be sure they aren't aware of what's happening."

"She's a prostitute. Doesn't serve any purpose for this world. Imagine how many men she's fucked over the years." Mal's face crinkles in disgust as he adds, "Vile bitch."

Whilst Mal's busy checking over his *patient,* I glance over at Sara. She's undone her leg clasp and shuffled a few feet across the room to my side. One of her hands is resting on the edge of my mattress, directly above where I hid my blade.

She seems intent on making a move, even if the plan seems half-considered at best. I mouth the word *vent* and turn back around. With one hand behind my back, I gesture the flicking of a lighter, hoping she catches on to my makeshift idea.

Once Tina is completely motionless, Mal declines the chair until Tina lies parallel to the floor. He continues with his incision, cutting a line neatly along the bottom left rib, extending out from the sternum.

"There's going to be some blood soon, among other leakage. So have a surgical sponge ready."

I do as he says, grabbing a couple of thin, translucent towels from the cart and placing them on Tina's legs. I don't want to partake in this, but if I can ensure the girl's survival, then it's something I must do.

A second, deeper cut exposes all the layers of her skin. I grimace at the sight of the yellowish fat. Mal pauses, as if he's unsure what to do next. He runs his fingers down the opening, smiling as he touches the exposed flesh. After contemplating for a minute, he gently tugs at both sides of the cut, pulling the gap wider.

"We're going to need retractors to keep the skin tissue pulled apart."

"What?"

"Those scissor looking things there," Mal says, pointing them out. "Grab two pairs."

If it wasn't for the situation, I could almost be fooled into thinking Mal had studied medicine. He talks a good game, anyway. I take a hold of the tools, trying to figure out how they work. Similar to regular scissors, they have rounded handles. However, the blade of the retractor scissors is much longer and narrower, with curved tips.

"Now take them and pull away the skin so I get a good view of her sternum," he instructs, licking his lips.

"You really enjoy this, don't you?"

"It's fascinating, the human body. Don't you think?"

I ignore him, clasping the first pair of scissors against the soft tissue of the skin, pulling it back as carefully as possible.

"These aren't the best for the job. The ones I wanted to get were slightly out of budget." The way Mal says it makes it sound like he's embarrassed, afraid to get judged for his low-cost choice of retractors.

"I'm sure they'll do the job well enough," I say, barely hiding a heavy dose of sarcasm.

A minute into the *procedure,* my hand begins shaking. With the mild sedative in my system, even holding a pair of scissors in place proves to be a struggle. Mal instructs me to use the second pair to grab onto the other side of the girl's skin. I have to move behind Tina, hovering over her head while I work. At least it looks like she's not present. The thought of the poor girl being aware of what was happening makes me sick.

Mal takes a deep breath, grabbing a drill from the lower compartment of the trolley. "I'm going to cut down the center now."

As the blade meets the bone with at a high-pitched grinding noise, I wince. It's not dissimilar to what I hear during infrequent dentist visits. I try to look away, but a sudden and unexpected thrill overtakes me. Seeing the anatomy of the human body up close, fascination surpasses my lingering disgust. I focus on the bone, watching it gradually break into two as Mal works his way up and down the center of the sternum.

Mal's voice hits my eardrum, breaking me out of my focus. He looks visibly uneasy. Does he care about the prospect of killing his patient prematurely, after all? "Grab the surgical sponge. We need to soak up the blood." Mal takes over one retractor while I shove the sponge under the girl's flesh. The white of the cloth quickly soaks through.

"What's next?" I ask.

"The final step," he says. "We pull the sternum apart to expose the heart."

"With our hands?"

"Yes, with our fucking hands. I don't have the correct tools for it."

"It's okay, keep your cool." I shove another sponge into another bloody pool and push it under Tina's skin.

We both let go of the retractors, leaving them clasped to the girl's flesh, and dig in around her breastbone. My fingers feel strange sensations—firm, yet spongy muscle, lumpy fat, elastic connective tissue. Sensations my fingers have never felt before. I'm hit with a surge of dopamine, to which I feel guilty, yet I'm drawn towards this girl's exposed chest cavity. It's a heady yet sickening feeling, like smoking too much dope. Or like watching a terrifying horror film through your fingers, unable to look away.

Mal gives me a nod. We pull at the breastbone, revealing what looks like large blood vessels and the top of her lungs. A large cracking sound stops me immediately. I recoil, worried I might've used too much force.

"Careful now," Mal says calmly. "Look," he points. There it is, nestled behind the sternum and ribcage—the heart. I watch its muscular walls contracting and relaxing with each heartbeat in fascination.

"It's beautiful," I say, with a surge of amazement.

Mal smiles. "Feel it," he instructs.

I do so without question, feeling the rhythmic pulsation against my fingertips. It's warm, smooth, somewhat slippery. We share a strange connection, with my heart beating to the rhythm of hers. I wipe my hand against the fabric of my jeans, while Mal caresses the heart himself, his face ridged with orgasmic pleasure.

"Isn't the human body fascinating?" he says.

I can only nod in agreement.

Mal gives me a pat on the back. "Alright, let's close her up now." He excitedly takes out a surgical stapler, like a child displaying their favorite toy. "She'll be as good as new," he says, pushing her skin together. After he's inserted two dozen staples, I release a deep breath, thankful that the girl is still breathing.

"She'll be okay?" I ask.

"I promise."

A sudden whiff of a burning smell hits my nostrils. I turn to see thick, black smoke coming from the vent above our mattresses, and Sara, standing with the dinner knife gripped in her hand.

"What have you done!?" Mal screams from the top of his lungs, running towards her.

I scramble to my senses, throwing my body forward and grabbing Mal by the feet. He falls down, bashing his head against the floor.

I lock eyes with Sara, and mouth the word *run*. She makes a dash for the ladder just as Mal kicks me in the face, drawing blood. I pull myself forward, grabbing both of his feet again, coiling myself against them as tightly as possible. Two words replay in my mind on a loop—*save Sara*. Nothing else matters, and the pain of his kicks barely registers. I clamp my eyes shut but sense Sara scampering across the room, taking hold of the ladder.

Mal and I break into coughing fits as the black smoke envelops the room, and he stops hitting me. I can't breathe, but it doesn't matter. I am choking, but it doesn't matter. My eyes open. Amid the chaos, I catch Sara looking over her shoulder at me from the ladder steps. She is beautiful. Poor, sweet Olivia.

I smile, knowing that I'll never see her again. Not in this life.

Razor blades fill my throat and I cannot speak. Instead, I mouth the words, "I love you."

"Let go of me!" Mal rasps between racking coughs. I instruct my weakened body to not let go. No matter how loud he screams, no matter how decrepit my body is. My only remaining function in this universe is to stop him from leaving this basement.

"This is the end of our little family," I whisper, watching as Sara unlocks the hatch and climbs out of sight. "How does it feel?"

Mal's fists batter my arms, my head, wherever he can reach. My eyes begin to swell shut from the blows, and my world becomes flashing shapes and colors.

With a bright light shining overhead, I see Sally reaching out her hand, calling me to join her now that I have completed my task. I have saved her. I have saved my little girl. *See, Olivia, I'm not giving up on you. We will see the sun again.*

"Hank." Mal's weak voice calls out to me in the dark, smoke-filled room. His blows have ceased, and we both lie intertwined, choking and gasping like fish left on the jetty. "We both know you belong here. You're not going to find peace out there in the world. There's nobody waiting for you. But here... here you have me, you have Sara."

"Sara is gone," I croak. The mattress smolders on, toxic smoke billowing around the room. We both lay with our faces pressed to the cold floor where the last oxygen remains.

"I know how you feel about her now, Hank. Out there you're a nobody, a goddamn truck driver. But with me, you could be a king. Remember that. We can start again, somewhere else."

Mal stops thrashing around. I let go of his legs and crawl my way over his body. When I reach his face, he's unconscious. I contemplate whether it was really him speaking, or if I'm imagining things.

The hatch above may as well be a million miles away—the summit of K2—but the door to the butchery is still ajar. I push it open with my feet and crawl back to Mal, then grab hold of the legs of his jeans, hauling him inch by inch towards the open door. My lungs spasm and wheeze. The agony in my chest eases as I cross the threshold into the butchery, where only a light haze of foul smoke has found its way in. With fresh oxygen in my lungs, I heave Mal across the threshold. Once his butt is onto the slick tiles, he's easier to move, and with my last remaining strength I haul myself upright, stumbling back into the smoke-filled basement.

I grab the chair, with Tina still prostrate on it. I'm not sure if she's still breathing. My vision is too hazy to tell. After I wheel her through to the butchery, and pull the door shut behind us, an overwhelming dizziness clouds me and my legs give out, sending me tumbling backwards onto Mal.

***

When I emerge from the depths of sheer nothingness, my lungs are raw, and my throat is drier than I can ever recall. All I know is that I need water. I reach out for the metal table in front of me and lever myself to my feet, nearly collapsing straight back down. Once a vicious headrush subsides, I step over Mal and stumble to the sink, turning the tap on full and gulping down mouthful upon mouthful of glorious water until my stomach is too full to contain any more.

With cupped hands, I splash more water onto my face and feel my strength returning with each handful. My mind and conscience clear, my body filled with the strength of a young man, I turn to appraise the two motionless bodies in the room with me. Before I can check them over, I push my hand against the butchery door. It is still cold. I push it open an inch. The room is smoky and stinks like a tire fire, but the blaze had little to feast on. It has blackened the ceiling above, but the building did not catch fire. If it had, I would never have awoken to know about it.

How long was I out? Sara will have found someone by now, and the police might be on their way. I check on Tina. Her chest isn't moving. Her face has the waxy pallor I know so well. It is a pity, but I know I am not to blame.

Mal will pay for it. I will make sure of that.

I loosen Tina's straps, place my hands underneath her body, and roll her off the chair. She flops facedown onto the hard floor with a dull *thunk,* like sandbags thrown from a truck.

My attention turns to Mal. I link my arms around his chest and haul him into an upright position, then put one arm underneath the backs of his knees and brace myself. With much grunting and straining, I manage to deadlift him, so I am standing with him cradled in my arms, before I place him gently onto the surface Tina was lying on. Once I have cut through his shirt and exposed his chest, I secure him with the straps. He moans and murmurs, slowly coming around. This doesn't startle me. Instead, I find myself grinning with satisfaction.

Show time.

21

Having wheeled over the cart from the other room and shut and locked the door behind me, I'm ready to begin.

"Rather than doing this the *proper* way, let's just have *fun*, shall we?" I say, eyeing all the silver tools at my disposal. My hand brushes over the scalpel, then the drill. "No, this won't do. We need a warmup."

Looking down at my fingerless hand, I figure that getting even only seems fair. I walk over to the tool-covered wall, scrutinizing each option. My eyes catch sight of a meat tenderizer hammer. "Never had one of those back home—let's see how it works."

I grab hold of it and walk back over to Mal. I observe his face for a moment, somehow still smug looking despite him being unconscious. We've got to change that. My arm retracts back, then comes down with full force, smashing into the back of his hand. The sound of shattering bones puts a wide smile on my face.

His eyes shoot wide open a split-second after impact, his shrieking cry filling the basement. Mal tries to raise the hand up, only to find himself completely immobile, helpless. I watch as his eyes desperately try to make sense of what's happening—eyeing the restraints, his battered hand, then me.

Before he has a chance to say a word, I instinctively drive the hammer down onto the same hand again, just in case there was a bone that hasn't shattered from my first blow.

His second scream is amped up by a few decibels. "What's the matter, Mal?" I joke, "Something wrong with your hand?"

No time to waste when the police could already be on their way. I do not want this party to be shut down before the last dance. I walk back towards the wall, dropping the hammer to the ground. "So many options," I mutter, eyeing up my next toy. But his screaming is getting on my nerves. I can't concentrate.

I take off one of my socks and force it into his mouth. He's still trying his best to voice his pain, but the noise isn't too bad now. Hearing his agony and watching him squirm gives me the perfect idea. I rummage through the cart until I find his stitching equipment—the ones he used to sew the back of my head up.

"Never done this before, so it'll be a bit of an experiment. Hope you don't mind."

Mal wriggles his head frantically from side to side when he sees me approaching with a curved needle and surgical stitches. I give him a disapproving shake of my head and a little tut before smacking him in the face. But this only seems to make him rattle around even more.

"This isn't going to work if you keep moving about like that," I warn him. He tries saying something, but the words are incoherent. "Sorry Mal, but I can't understand what you're saying. You've got a sock in your mouth." What I can tell, though, is that he's not scared, at least not scared enough for me to feel satisfied. I put down the needle and stitches, replacing them with a drill. Need to put a little more fear into him before continuing.

I point the drill down towards his thigh, then press down on the trigger switch. Mal's muffled cries drown out the drill's high-pitched squeal as it tears through his flesh. I don't stop even when the drill has gone all the way through. I let it continue rotating, hopefully mangling up his innards. My eyes remain locked with his while I savor his pain.

His blue jeans change to red as the blood soaks through. I only stop after another minute with the drill, then I give him another whack across the face for good measure. He doesn't show any signs of calming down, so when I pick up the needle again, I stand behind the chair and lock his head in my arms to stop him from moving.

"Shh, shh, don't move around," I whisper, still gripping his head tightly on both sides. Before he thrashes about again, I slide the needle through his top lip. He tries jerking his head in response, but I maintain my hold, continuing to push the needle until it goes through the bottom lip as well.

"Good job Mal, stay still for me." I work my way back up, piercing through both lips again. I have to admit—he still has plenty of fight left. Each time he tries to resist, I jab him in the face. One of my punches accidentally connects with the side of his nose, opening the floodgates. I try closing his nostrils to stop the bleeding but quickly realize that he's unable to breathe through his mouth. I break out into manic laughter, watching him panic.

"Silly me," I confess, letting the blood flow down his face. I grip his head once more and repeat the stitching until I've made it all the way to the end of his mouth. When I stand back to observe, I admit to myself that I didn't do a *great* job with the stitching, but hey, it's my first time.

"Now, why don't we just get to the good part," I announce, grabbing a sharp scalpel from the trolley. I think back to how he used it on Tina, surgically making an incision down the center of her chest, and try to picture the exact process Mal followed.

"This might sting a little," I say, pressing down on his soft skin tissue with the top of the scalpel. The initial cut is only small, yet bright red blood flows down his skin in an instant. Mal squirms, wriggling about like a fish. His eyes look like they're screaming—this only amplifies my enjoyment. The stitches give way slightly, but with the sock in his mouth, all he does is cause himself more pain.

I press down with the scalpel once more, only stopping when I reach the top of his stomach. It's impossible to even see the incision with the amount of blood pouring out. My forearm acts like a windshield wiper, smearing the blood all over the place, but the longer I spend clearing the blood, the more gushes out.

Can't delay—I grab the bloody drill, give Mal a smile and grind his sternum to bits. It's a real mess. I'm not anywhere near as good as Mal is at surgery. He certainly doesn't seem to be enjoying it. He pulls his head back, his eyes tightly shut whilst he voices his pain. I don't stop until I stop feeling bone obstructing my entrance. By this time, Mal's beginning to shake violently like something out of *The Exorcist*.

I chuck the drill to the side and force my arm into his chest, feeling around for his heart. Inside, it's warm, wet. Everything around me is moving around like fish in a pond. Bits of scattered bone jab into my hand, but a little pain is nothing I can't handle after all that he's done to me.

A calmness washes over me when I wrap my fingers around its coarse texture, feeling its violent beats. Once I have savored the shock of realization written onto Mal's face, I grip it tighter, and yank it. The blood vessels stretch, working against me, pulling it back like a rubber band. I grimace, pulling at it with greater and greater force, giving it all my strength. Finally, the surrounding tissue gives way with an audible snap, and I rip the still-beating heart from its roots.

I tower over Mal's twitching body, his bloody heart pulsating in my hand, gushing jets of dark blood across the room, and painting his shock-frozen face. I give it a squeeze, letting its juices drip down onto the slick floor before I bring it to my mouth and clamp my eyes shut in exquisite expectation. My tongue curls around the warm muscle, and I bite down, causing an explosion of flavor to burst inside my mouth.

Bon appétit.

Printed in Great Britain
by Amazon

45194899R00148